COYOTE REVENGE

FRED HARRIS

AVON BOOKS
An Imprint of HarperCollinsPublishers

This is a work of fiction. Names, characters, places, and incidents are products of the author's imagination or are used fictitiously and are not to be construed as real. Any resemblance to actual events, locales, organizations, or persons, living or dead, is entirely coincidental.

AVON BOOKS
An Imprint of HarperCollins*Publishers*
10 East 53rd Street
New York, New York 10022-5299

First Avon Books paperback printing: October 2000
First HarperCollins hardcover printing: November 1999

Avon Trademark Reg. U.S. Pat. Off. and in Other Countries, Marca Registrada, Hecho en U.S.A.
HarperCollins ® is a trademark of HarperCollins Publishers Inc.

Printed in the U.S.A.

❖ 10 9 8 7 6 5 4 3 2 1

Praise for
COYOTE REVENGE

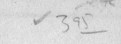

"Harris gives us a refreshing, artful addition to the themes mystery writers play—plus an authentic look at how life was in rural America in the depth of the Depression."

Tony Hillerman

"It doesn't take long for Fred Harris to pull us into the tough-luck world of *Coyote Revenge* . . . . [Harris] writes in a bone-dry style that's made to order for his Dust Bowl setting."

New York Times Book Review

"A remarkably precise and textured portrait. . . . What sets this novel apart is the dead-on dialogue, rich array of characters, and concise narrative."

Chicago Tribune

"Evocative. . . . Harris displays a solid prose style. His dialect is particularly well wrought, and he delivers . . . effective scenes."

Publishers Weekly

"A promising debut."
San Diego Union Tribune

"A lively storyteller with a keen eye for the people and the language of that era. . . . *Coyote Revenge* would make a good movie. Robert Duvall would be perfect."
Tulsa World

"The writing is simple and clear. The characters are interesting. The hero is appropriately complex."
Albuquerque Journal

Other Books by Fred Harris

Easy Pickin's

Coming Soon in Hardcover

To my sister, Sue.
Like so many Oklahomans, she knows how
to tough it out when times get hard.
And to my wife, Margaret Elliston,
the kindly muse.

I am grateful to Laura Harris and Sue Stauffer for historical research, to Dr. Dayton Voorhees and Dr. Malcolm Sher for medical advice, and to Geneva Navarro for her help with the Comanche language. Many thanks, too, to Kathryn Harris Tijerina, Margaret Elliston, and Laura Harris, again, for reading the manuscript and offering helpful suggestions. And I appreciate the critically valuable help of David Stewart Hull, my agent, as well as the excellent guidance of Vice President and Associate Publisher Gladys Justin Carr and Associate Editor Erin Cartwright, my wonderful editors at Harper-Collins.

*T*he first bullet ruined Hoyt Ready's heart, and he was dead before the quick second one came. He never saw the killer, never heard the killer, either.

Hoyt Ready hadn't heard the kitchen screen door open. He didn't hear the floor creak as the killer came stealthily from the kitchen into the living room–dining room of the well-kept, white-frame, two-story farmhouse. The Readys lived out in the country, half a mile west and half a mile north of Cash County's Essaquahnahdale School and nearly a half mile from nearest neighbors.

There had been no car noise when the killer arrived. Ready's wife, Inez, upstairs changing clothes, would have heard that for sure. The killer had parked in a WPA-built American-elm-and-black-locust windbreak 150 yards west and had walked to the house.

The Readys were just back from Sunday morning services at the First Methodist Church in Vernon, the southwest Oklahoma county seat, where Hoyt ran the bank. Inez, middle-aged, prim, and thin as a praying mantis, clunked in her heavy black dress shoes up the stairs to their bedroom to take off her black-crepe Sunday dress and put on a wraparound workday smock.

Downstairs, Hoyt Ready took off his black suit coat, opened the closet door next to the framed color print of the Last Supper, and hung the coat neatly on a wooden hanger he found there. Hoyt liked everything neat and in its place. He also liked to eat on time, and he was used to being boss.

"Jesus Christ, Inez!" he hollered up the stairs. "I hope you're not going to take all day on putting out dinner."

She came to the head of the stairs, and called down, "I left it in the oven, warming. Won't take a minute after I get my clothes changed."

"What?" Hoyt yelled. As a child in Kansas, he'd suffered a high fever that had left his hearing impaired.

Inez didn't answer. Hoyt picked up the weekly Vernon Herald from the table and pulled a straight-backed oak dining chair over to the west window. He pushed the ivory-colored lace curtains apart to get a better light, then sat down facing toward the narrow, steep stairs, his back to the kitchen.

The small-town banker hadn't even finished reading the lead front-page story of the local weekly's latest edition—a story headlined, "Oklahoma 1935 Farm Foreclosures Reach All-Time High"—when the killer poked the barrel of the semiautomatic .22-caliber rifle through the chair back's rungs, almost touching the cloth of the starched white shirt, fired point-blank, then quickly fired again. Neither bullet exited.

Hoyt Ready's body slumped forward, shirt back reddening. Brilliantined black hair, which he combed from low on the left side over a spreading bald spot, fell down over his eyes. The killer reached to pull the body back to keep it in the chair.

"What was that?" Inez said loudly, alarmed, as she came hurriedly down the stairs barefoot, tying her flowered cotton smock in front. "Hoyt?"

She came to a quick stop at the bottom of the stairs as she saw her dead husband in the chair, head lolling to one side, and at the same time took in the person with the gun standing behind him. Her eyes went wide. She put her hand over her mouth. But she didn't cry out. It was almost as if she had been expecting something like this.

The killer looked her squarely in the face. Neither said anything during the instant it took the killer to take two quick steps forward and shoot her in the left breast.

Inez Ready sat down heavily on the top step. She looked down at the rapidly spreading bright red patch of blood on her smock front, and then rolled over on her knees, as if to pray.

"Oh, Lord, I'm dead," she said.

"Not yet," the killer said grimly, taking another step toward the wounded woman and deliberately placing a second shot midway up on the left side of her back. The woman slumped face forward onto the stairs. Now, sure enough dead.

Not rushing, the killer leaned the rifle against a wall and went carefully about arranging things. The Readys were made to sit, side by side, at the dining table. It wasn't hard putting them there. Hoyt Ready was small and lean. He weighed little more than his wife, always having preached that overeating was a sin.

The kitchen screen door banged once and soon banged again, as the killer exited and quickly reentered with a red five-gallon can of kerosene, or coal oil, as people called it.

The rag rug that Inez Ready had made herself, the tablecloth she'd crocheted, and the off-white lace curtains she'd hemmed by hand for the room's two windows—all these were drenched. The last gallon of kerosene was splashed over the Readys' heads and shoulders.

The killer dropped the kerosene can just inside the kitchen screen door, then took a box of matches from the kitchen counter. Using four matches, the killer carefully set fire to the curtains at the two windows, then the table-top, and, finally, the rug beneath the table.

Outside again, the killer waited a full minute to be

sure the flames were catching fully. They were. Turning then, the killer began to jog toward the secreted vehicle, knowing that there was not the slightest possibility that the nearest volunteer fire departments—Vernon's, five miles north, or Wardell's, five and a half miles east— would receive an alarm and get to the farmhouse until well after everything had been reduced to charcoal.

ONE

Old Sore-eyed Cecil and two of his ragged little girls were on the corner in front of the bank, braced against a stiff early-November wind. He heard my cowboy boots on the sidewalk and held out a thin hand. I fished a dime out of my Levi's and gave it to him as I passed.

"Lord bless you," he said.

"I hope He's quick," I said.

Not to Sore-eyed Cecil.

I started up the five semicircular concrete steps to the bank's etched-glass front door. I was a walking prayer myself, a climbing supplication. And nervous as a whore in church, my dad would have said.

Cash County National Bank was a kind of green-back temple in Vernon, Oklahoma, something like a church. It weighted down the northwest corner of Icehouse and Main Streets and was the commanding structure of the town's five-block central business district. On Main Street, two drugstores, two cafés, two picture shows, two dry goods stores, two furniture stores, three groceries, a variety store, a hardware store, three car dealerships, a jewelry, a ladies' dress store, a bakery, a hole-in-the-wall radio-repair shop, two lumberyards, three blacksmith shops, and four beer joints that sold 3.2 beer, the only legal liquor allowed by Oklahoma state law, and, on the northwest edge of town, two cotton gins and a grain elevator—these were the Vernon businesses that had survived hard times or replaced those that didn't. Four vacant storefronts on Main Street were the tombs of enterprises the Depression had killed off for good.

Several of Vernon's downtown buildings were two stories tall. Their second floors housed the offices of four lawyers, five insurance and real-estate agents, two dentists, and three chiropractors. The names and occupations of these professionals were lettered in black or gold on the windows looking down on the asphalt north–south thoroughfare of the town.

Cash County National Bank, itself, was two-story. It was a red-brick cube of a building, in no danger of ever being scooped up by a southwest Oklahoma tornado or carried off in one of the terrible dust storms that had nearly blown us away after the start of the "dirty thirties." The bank was too solid and heavy for that. And besides, I figured, God wouldn't have dared.

The bank wasn't going to go under financially, either. It'd been making money during the hard times.

I took a nervous breath at the top of the steps, squared my shoulders, turned the brass doorknob, and entered the well-lit, high-ceilinged inner sanctum. Times were getting better, that fall of 1937, but the Great Depression was definitely still on. And I needed to borrow some money.

Marsh Traynor saw me right away when I entered. His desk was in an alcove to the left as you came in. Farther toward the rear, three brass-grilled tellers' cells were backed up against the north and west walls.

"Okie!" Traynor hollered, getting up out of his chair. "Come in this house!" My dad always said, "Marsh Traynor don't talk; he bellers!" He was right.

Red-faced and bald as a melon, Traynor was built like a heavyweight wrestler. But he looked spry as a vaulter as he jumped out from behind his oak desk and came quickly to the low oak rail, bending briefly to open its latched gate. The right hand he grabbed mine with felt nearly as thick as an eight-ounce boxing glove. His other hand gripped my shoulder, and he pulled me off-balance, toward him, in a near embrace.

"Right good to see you, Okie," Traynor yelled. "Right good." He stepped back then. "Come in, come in," he said in a somewhat quieter voice, motioning me through the low gate to one of the two unpadded oak office chairs in front of the desk. He went around and sat down in his own worn, brown-leather chair.

On the wall behind his desk was a twice life-size black-and-white, framed photograph of President Franklin Delano Roosevelt's strong and confident face. He'd been reelected for a second term by a landslide the preceding year.

The only thing I have to fear is fear itself, I thought to myself, adapting Roosevelt's words.

Traynor had enthusiastically backed Roosevelt, I knew. I also knew that this had been a singular thing for an Oklahoma banker to do. But it matched the common sentiment in Cash County, for sure. My dad, for example, about as common as they came, liked to say, "When Roosevelt took his seat in '33, we commenced to climb, and we clumb!"

Traynor didn't look like a banker. Didn't dress like

one either. And the fact was that he hadn't actually been a banker very long—only since old man Ready, a different person altogether, a tightfisted and sour-turned Methodist deacon, and his wife, both Republicans, had been found dead in their burned-down farmhouse a couple of years earlier. Few people had mourned Ready's death. He'd foreclosed on a sadly large number of Cash County farmers after the Depression struck, running them off their home places. Some of these dispossessed had gone off to California, looking for work. Most of them were still around Vernon, many on relief.

Traynor wore a leather jacket and an open-necked, blue work shirt. And, most unusual for a banker, his round, permanently sun-reddened face was lit by a near-perpetual smile.

My dread about coming to the bank was a kind of holdover feeling from Hoyt Ready's days there. When I was a kid, I'd sometimes tagged along when my dad went in to see Ready, and I'd watched my dad change the minute he walked through the bank's front doors. A wiry cowboy kind of a guy with a busted nose, my dad was as tough as a tire iron and not much bigger. But, going to see the banker, he'd always seemed to me to weaken and even to shrink a little. He'd take off his worn Stetson and drop his eyes, like a guy going through a cow lot, careful where he stepped.

It was true that my dad, as he put it, "wore no man's collar," but he came pretty close to buckling one on every time he went to the bank during the time Ready ran it.

Hoyt Ready was from Kansas. My dad called it the state of the three suns—"sunshine, sunflowers, and sunsabitches."

"Bastard acts like it gives him a case of the piles to have to loan you a little money," my dad said about

Ready. This was true, even though, as people learned after he died, Ready had owned virtually no personal interest in the bank. He was an employee, chinchy with another guy's money. The actual owner lived up in Oklahoma City. That's the man Marsh Traynor, newly rich as an oil wildcatter, had bought the bank from immediately after Hoyt Ready's death.

"How are you, sir?" I said.

"Cut the 'sir' shit, Okie," Traynor roared. "Try 'Marsh.'"

I shouldn't have been so nervous, but I really needed the money. I'd known Traynor since I was a kid. He was no silver-spoon guy. I'd baled hay for him, working in my dad's baler crew, when Traynor was still trying to make a living on an upland farm and bootlegging on the side. Everybody in Cash County knew that selling whiskey was the way he'd put together enough money to buy an old spudder rig and start wildcatting.

Traynor'd first drilled shallow wells west of Vernon. Then, offsetting from the rich Burkburnett, Texas, field, he'd put down a deeper well just on this side, the Oklahoma side, of Red River—over in the southwest corner of Cash County. And that's when he'd hit it big.

"You lookin' good, Okie," Traynor bawled. "Still make a hunnerd and forty-seven pound, if you had to."

"Broke guys don't put on much," I said.

Traynor was right about my weight. I knew because I was wearing the same pair of Levi's and the same white dress shirt I'd worn, back when I'd fought welterweight, right out of high school. I'd stayed in shape.

Traynor pulled a cloth Bull Durham sack and a small packet of cigarette papers from his blue work shirt's left pocket. He took out and held a thin sheet in his left hand, sifted the tobacco into it with his right, then deftly rolled the paper up and licked it as a seal. He closed the tobacco sack by pulling on its drawstrings with his teeth and proffered it and the papers to me. I shook my head. Traynor took a kitchen match out of his khaki pants pocket, struck it with his right thumbnail, and, cupping the flame like he was out in the wind, lit up. He inhaled deeply and blew the smoke out his nose.

"Still fightin' any, since you been up at the university?" he blared.

"Not and getting paid for it," I said. "Not since Cameron College, you know—after I got back from Long Beach and Mexico."

"Speck they ain't much money in it," Traynor said. "What'd you pick up the night you and old man Nahnahpwa's boy fought to a draw, here at the Murray Theater—what's that boy's name, killed in a car wreck?"

"Marvin," I said.

"Best God dern prizefight I ever seen."

"We split six bucks," I said. "Not much, but I was glad to get it; I was chopping cotton, along then, for a dollar a day."

"Make any pesos fightin' them Mesakins?" Traynor wanted to know.

"A little," I said. I'd traveled the boxing circuit in Mexico for half a year, before coming back to Oklahoma for college.

"Fought about as much outside the ring as in. Places like Mexicali and Guanajuato, had to fight the local manager to get my winnings. A few other places, practically had to fight my way out of the arena. People came to see the gringo get beat, even if they had to do it themselves."

I cleared my throat. "And money's what I came to talk with you about, Mr. Traynor—Marsh," I said. "I need to borrow a hundred and fifty dollars to buy an old bobtail '35 Chevy truck off of Fat Rogers. And I need a line of credit, something like another couple of hundred, so I can go to trading cattle."

Cow traders bought directly from farmers, or at weekly auctions in Vernon and nearby towns, and resold—for a profit, if the traders were any good, and they didn't last long if they weren't—at the stockyards in Oklahoma City. The Oklahoma cattle market had come back in the last year or so.

"Had to drop out of law school at Norman, your dad told me."

"They tin-canned me out of town, my last year," I said. "I wasn't raised to be a quitter, but I was broke. Couldn't save up enough last summer, tabling broom corn and following the wheat threshing up north."

It was as good an explanation as any, although it didn't account for my leaving school in midsemester. But Traynor didn't know that.

"My dad started me out trading cattle when I was practically a kid," I said. "It's something I know, and I think I can make a living at it. After a year or so, I still hope to go back to school."

"Hudge has done all right, tradin'—smart as a whip," Traynor said.

"It's about all my dad's ever done, that and custom haybaling," I said. "He's not one for 'workin' for the other feller,' as he puts it."

"I never had no better friend than old Hudge," Traynor said. "He'll do to tie to."

"You know, I moved in with him after I came back this week—out at the old Billings place on the east edge of town," I said. "Just me and him. He's been baching there since Mama had her stroke and passed away a little over a year ago."

"It was right sad about your mother," Traynor

said, his voice quieter. "Opal was one of God's good women. Hudge drankin'?"

"Not as much as he was, I don't think," I said. I was shading the truth again.

"Okie, I'm gonna let you have the money." He waved off my thanks. "Write a check for the truck and bring me the title. I'll treat you like your dad on tradin'. I'll cover your check each time you buy a load of cattle, and you deposit your commission-house check when you sell 'em in the City."

"I'm much obliged," I said.

"How old are you, Okie?"

"Not quite twenty-six, sir."

Traynor rubbed his hand over his bald head. "Well, you're a good risk. You was a rugged football player and a dern tough boxer. You always worked hard, and you got a head on your shoulders. You oughta partner up some with old Stud Wampler. He and your dad are about the brainiest cow traders they is."

"I hope to, some."

Traynor sat up straight in his chair and looked me sternly in the eye. "And, now, don't go and fall in again with that sumbitch, Dub Ready. You seen him since you got back?"

"Not to talk to."

"He's the high sheriff, now, you know—wearin' a badge and totin' a gun." Traynor's tone was sarcastic.

I said I knew. I did. But one thing I did not know then was that I, myself, would soon pin on that same badge.

"Folks elected me a county commissioner after I bought the bank," Traynor said. "Money makes you respectable—and popular, too." His voice was a bellow again, and the two tellers and a customer in the lobby turned to look at him, but he went right on.

"So, I'm forced to deal with your old runnin' buddy, Dub. He's as slick as greased owl shit, and he ain't got no more use for the law than a hog does a sidesaddle. Watch him, Okie; he may be young, but the way he operates is gettin' pretty old."

"I will," I said.

But Traynor wouldn't turn loose of it. "The sumbitch tried to put the screws to me." He was still talking in a near roar, and there was a sharp edge of malice in his voice. "But he's about to get his. It won't be long, neither."

I hardly had time to puzzle over what he might mean by this ominous-sounding prediction before he changed the subject.

"And what about Juanita?" Traynor asked. I was glad he'd lowered his voice some. "Seen her? She came back a little over two years ago, short while before their folks burned up."

"No, sir, haven't seen Juanita in seven years," I said. "Not since right after the class of '30 got our diplomas and old man Ready hustled her off to St. Louis."

There was no need to say any more about that. Vernon was a small town. People knew. I didn't care to say any more about it, either. The mention of Juanita's name still put a sick ache in my chest, like when you get hit a hard lick over the heart.

I changed the subject. "The Readys killed themselves, they say."

"'Course, most people hated old Hoyt like a weed," Traynor said. "And I was one of 'em."

"How come?" I asked.

"Mean bastard foreclosed on my old daddy and put him in his grave," Traynor bellowed. "He'da waited just a month, my daddy woulda found out there was oil on his place and paid out. Ready must have known about the oil, why he moved so fast.

Later on, tried to foreclose on me, too. And Inez
Ready, just as mean as Hoyt, and then some, I
reckon. God knows they was both meaner'n old
Billy Hell to them kids, flat drove 'em off. But no
question it was a bad thang, anyway, the way they
died. Hoyt and Inez was still livin' at the old home
place, south of town, you know—half a mile west
and half a mile north of 'Squahnahdale School.

"Accordin' to the report, they set a-fire to the
house and then killed their ownselves," Traynor
went on. "Dub and Juanita heired what they had,
and, matter a course, run through it like a dose a
salts. She's as bad as her brother and wild as a
peach-orchard boar. Don't get mixed up with neither
one of 'em."

"I won't, sir," I said. I knew I was telling Traynor
a little something less than the full truth for the third
time in a row.

TWO

Two weeks later, Thursday, November 11, was a sunny fall day in Vernon. The radio said it was supposed to get up into the seventies. By ten o'clock, something over a thousand people thronged both sides of Main Street, waiting for the Armistice Day parade to begin.

They were dressed in the best shopping-day clothes they had, which for many were none too good. What a lot of people wore looked as used as their hard faces, though the freshly ironed, faded blue overalls of the men and boys and the small-figured, cotton print dresses of the women and girls showed vigorous, recent, and generous use of the brown and ugly, but serviceable, lye soap that the women had made at home.

A goodly number of these women wore dresses sewn from flour sacks. A lot of the kids wore too-loose or too-tight, hand-me-down shoes that they'd only put on since the fall weather had turned too cold for them to go barefooted any longer. Quite a few of the poorer kids had ringworm on their faces and boils on their necks, and some had water bumps or scratched sores on their hands from the seven-year itch.

I was jawing with the other cow traders, huddled up at our regular spot on the corner in front of Herschel Brothers Drug. It was where we met on weekday mornings before heading off to an auction sale or separately partnering up to go out and try to buy some farmer's cattle directly.

The crowd was all around us. I had on my cow trader's outfit: clean and well-ironed Levi's, a neat white dress shirt with abalone buttons, a black suit jacket, nicely shined-up black boots, and a comfortable old gray-white, medium-brimmed Stetson.

At law school, I'd dressed differently, of course. There, I'd worn gabardine slacks and a required coat and tie. My college mustache was long gone, too, and not just because my dad made fun of it. He called it a cookie duster or a French tickler.

"Uh-oh, Okie stud," Stud Wampler suddenly said, "look like you got yourself a haircut and forgot to say 'no rinctums.'" He made a quick reach to try to yank the newly short black hairs at the back of my head. It was an old school-ground boy's game.

Stud was stout and half a head taller than my five-ten, and he was about fifteen years older than me, too, but playful as a kid. I grasped him by his huge upper arms, but it wasn't easy to keep him away. We scuffled a little, and people moved aside from us.

"Quit," I said, "or I'm not gonna help you make any more money, like I did last week."

"Yeah, Stud," Fat Rogers said to Wampler from behind us. "Mess up you meal ticket, and you gonna have to go on welfare commodities."

"Heah, you boys!" my dad said, but not trying to separate us. "Straighten up, or I'll take my pocketknife to both ya'll."

We laughed, then, and stopped. I picked up my hat from the pavement and dusted it off.

"And, look yonder, anyway," my dad said. "The parade's commencin'."

It was. We heard the siren and pushed forward a little with the rest of the crowd in order to see better.

Two blocks north of us, Vernon's old caisson-tired, faded red Ferguson fire truck appeared around the courthouse corner to lead the procession down Main Street in our direction. The driver's helper hand-cranked the siren. Dogs howled. Old women held their ears. A ways back, horses of the Sheriff's Posse shied. Vernon's annual Armistice Day parade was under way.

It wasn't long before the fire truck passed in front of us, siren whining; behind it came a marching company of about thirty veterans of the Great War. Some had to work at keeping in step, kind of skipping or hopping now and then. Most were in their forties, the majority a little paunchy. Nearly all wore blue American Legion campaign caps and civilian clothes.

At the front of this group were two uncles of mine, my mother's brothers. They carried the Oklahoma and American flags and stepped along like drum majors. Uncle Joe Ray and Uncle Leroy Vanderwerth were as thin as hoe handles in their old doughboy uniforms, which still fit them. Neither one of them so much as shot us a quick glance as they passed. They were all business.

The uncles were from Wise County, Texas, like my mother. Before the war, they'd come to Vernon to live with my folks for a few years before the army drafted them. My real name, Ray Lee, came from a combination of theirs. But nobody much had ever called me that. My dad started calling me Okie because I was born on November 16, Oklahoma statehood day, and most everybody else had always done the same.

After the war, Uncle Joe Ray and Uncle Leroy had never again been quite right. They'd come back to Vernon shell-shocked, people called it, from what must have been something close to hell that they'd experienced in the trenches of France. They lived by themselves, bached, on an Indian-lease farm southeast of Vernon and got by the best they could—hunting and fishing, raising turkeys, selling cream and eggs, and making home-brew beer.

Behind the veterans in the Armistice Day parade came the well-mounted, about twenty-member, riding group that called itself the Cash County Sheriff's Posse. Their fine ponies, shod hooves clattering on the pavement, seemed almost to step in time to the loud strains of the traditional fight song, "On Old Vernon!" blared out by the blue-and-white-garbed Vernon High School band, which came quick-marching right behind them.

Dub Ready, of course, headed up the Posse, holding himself as proud as the sleek, dancing buckskin gelding he rode. He wore new Levi's with pressed creases, an elegant black-wool cowboy shirt with white piping around the cuffs and the double pockets, and a black-leather vest. He sat comfortably in the slightly squeaking brown leather of a like-new Western saddle with a big padded horn.

The reaction of the crowd showed that Dub was popular in Cash County. A continuous wave of light applause greeted him from both sides of the street as he passed along.

People called out to him approvingly, "Lookin' good, Sheriff."

"How's it goin', Dub."

And from time to time, he took off his black cowboy hat to acknowledge these friendly greetings, speaking to individual men here and there.

I thought there was no telling what the brown-alligator boots he wore might have cost. A heavy, tan-leather gun belt was strapped around his waist, and a big, pearl-handled Colt revolver rested snugly in the holster on his right hip.

As soon as he spied our group of cow traders on the Herschel Drug corner to his right, he reined over to us, out of the flow of the parade, and held his horse back.

"How you doin', Hudge . . . Stud . . . boys?" Dub said, smiling winningly, holding his hat. His wavy red hair was cut close and combed straight back from a high forehead. He sat the nervous horse easily, handsome as the Tom Mix he and I used to go to the picture shows together as kids to see.

"J. W.," my dad said.

"Stud," Stud Wampler said, his usual greeting for everybody. That's how he'd picked up his nickname. Nobody could remember when he'd started that, nor for that matter why he often talked in the whiny nasal tones of W.C. Fields.

"Dub," Fat Rogers said. The rest of us gave an understated nod, like we were bidding at a cow sale.

Dub jerked the reins to settle the gelding and sidled him over a little closer. "Back home, Okie," he said, looking directly at me for the first time.

"You've got an eagle eye, Dub, since turning lawman," I said. "I'm back."

"Expect you goin' to the program, Okie, down't auditorium," Dub said.

"Studyin' about it," I said.

"Let's me and you talk. Might could put you in the way of makin' some money."

Before I could react, Dub set his hat back on, winked, and fired a quick shot at me with his right forefinger, thumb coming down like a hammer.

Then he touched up the spirited buckskin and was
soon down the street and back at the front of the
Posse again.

I wanted to see Dub. But I had my doubts about
getting into any kind of deal with him.

A little way back from the Posse and the Vernon
band came another horseback group—about a
dozen, mostly older, Comanche Indians in braids
and full-fringed deerskin and beaded costumes. Old
man Nahnahpwa and his wife, Lucy, were in front.
Most of the Indians rode Western-style saddles. But
the old man and his wife rode bareback, like in the
old days, except for the gray Navajo blanket spread
over the back of his black pony and the red one on
her paint. They weren't using bridles, either. Instead,
in the Comanche way, they were guiding with knee
pressure on the horses' ribs and neck-reining them
with braided-rawhide lariats, one end in their left
hands, the other end looped tight around the horses'
lower jaws.

Nahnahpwa's face was a smooth swatch of
tanned leather—no eyebrows, eyelashes, or
whiskers. Comanche men plucked out all their facial
hair. For the parade, his cheeks were rouged, and he
wore silver, peyote-bird earrings dangling from each
of his large ears.

I caught the old man's eye, and he nodded as he
passed.

Twenty-eight county schools had student marching groups in the parade—ranging from town high
schools to one-room country schools. And there
were fourteen separate organization and school
floats, a few built on flatbed trucks, the rest on trail-
ers pulled by teams of horses or rubber-tired trac-
tors. Each of the floats was decorated with what
looked like a day's pay worth of primary-colored
crepe paper, and most of them wore dragging, wrap-

around cotton skirts of patriotic red, white, and blue bunting.

The crowd liked Wardell High School's "Flanders Field" float best. Built on a hay trailer and pulled by an olive green Oliver tractor, it was a green cemetery of fake funeral-parlor grass, bordered all around by a narrow bed of red-paper poppies. Two Wardell schoolgirls, dressed up as nurses, stood on each side of a wounded schoolboy soldier, his head wrapped in a bloodstained bandage. They held his arms and steadied him while he struggled to stand at attention as another schoolboy doughboy played a mournful, if sometimes problematic, taps on a raised bugle.

Toward the tail end of the procession came something like a thirty-horse, cowboy-costumed gang from the Vernon Rodeo Club. I made out Juanita in this bunch while they were still a half a block away.

You couldn't miss her. Tight, black riding pants and high-topped black cowboy boots. Black-leather jacket with a lot of fringe shaking on the sleeves. White cowgirl hat and white bandanna at the open neck of a black-taffeta blouse. Perfect, baking soda white complexion, thin nose, rosebud lips painted a brilliant Tangee red, a cascade of rich black hair that fell well past her shoulders in back. And she was riding a spectacular strawberry-roan mare with a long white mane and tail.

"Okie, you a mite sick?" my dad suddenly asked, taking hold of my arm and looking me intently in the face.

I realized, then, that I'd made an involuntary low noise and jerked a half step backward. I still felt a strong urge to try to fade into the crowd before she could see me.

"Heartburn," I said.

"Whut I figured."

She was right in front of me, then, expertly hold-

ing the impatient mare as other horses passed on by,
just as her brother had done.

"Heard you were back, Ray Lee—buying cows,"
she said, green eyes teasing. She still had the
alabaster face of Hedy Lamarr, the half-naughty
voice of Mae West. "Not interested in heifers?" She
didn't care what people who heard her thought.

"Didn't know, for sure, what was on the market."
I was more unsettled than I sounded.

"Come by and check it out," she said. She neck-
reined the roan mare around sharply, quickly
maneuvered back among the rodeo riders, and they
passed on down Main.

My dad and the cow traders knew better than to
try to kid me about her.

Behind the rodeo bunch, next to last in the
parade, came the Wardell High School band, smartly
dressed in black and gold and marching spiritedly to
their school song, "Tigers Will Roar Tonight."
Scattered cheers and applause from Wardell parti-
sans greeted them. And there were also a few sour
taunts from a knot of Vernon Junior High boys near
us. "Blow it out your bloomer leg!" one smart-aleck
kid yelled.

Cash County's only two towns of any size were
rivals—in football, basketball, and everything else.
Wardell's population amounted to about a thousand, compared to Vernon's fifteen hundred. Vernon
had the county courthouse, and Wardell resented
that. And it was a matter of some raillery in Vernon,
which dumped its raw sewage in nearby East Cash
Creek, that Wardell got its city water out of the same
stream, only ten miles farther south. A bit of graffiti
commonly scrawled over the commodes in Vernon
beer-joint toilets read: "Please flush. Wardell needs
water!"

Two walking legionnaires brought up the rear of the parade. They dragged a miniature, wheeled cannon, which they primed and fired periodically, about once a block. Each reverberating boom of the near-toy weapon echoed loudly up and down Main Street's shallow canyon and rattled the upstairs windows above the stores. People in the crowd held their ears at these concluding explosions and began to drift away as the cannon team passed.

Stud Wampler, my dad, Fat Rogers, and I decided to skip the live-turkey drop-off from the one-story roof of Mark's Bakery, a block south on Main. It was an event that always drew a big crowd, especially at a time when a lot of people came to town hungry, as they did in the thirties, lured by the right to take home any panicky, wing-flailing bird that they could catch and hold. The drop was an annual feature of Turkey Day, always observed in conjunction with Armistice Day in Vernon. The town proudly called itself the Turkey Capital of Oklahoma.

"Turkey shit and feathers ain't my idea of a good time, boys," my dad said.

The four of us turned in the other direction and stumped up Main Street toward Marshall's Cafe. It was half a block away. My dad bobbed up and down beside us on his gimp leg. But, as usual, there was enough of a forbidding and dangerous aura about him to make passersby avert their eyes and take no open notice of the odd way he walked.

At Marshall's, I held the door, and we stepped inside, where the air was, as usual, thick with cooking grease and you could always count on eating the best hamburger in Oklahoma, big as a plate, for a nickel.

THREE

"Ain't nair one of us feels like hearin' ol' Jesse sing 'Over There' again," my dad said, as we finished off our hamburgers and french fries at Marshall's. Nobody wanted to go with me to the Armistice Day program at the high school.

Jesse Dowlin, the judge from our two-county district, was a native of Cash County and a raspy tenor. Ever since he'd first been elected county clerk after coming back from the Great War, he could always be counted on to turn up, unannounced, at nearly every local box supper and pie supper and at a lot of school assemblies, too. He'd make a speech, then lead group singing. The judge was a veteran, and he favored songs from the war.

We got up from the table, put on our hats, and joined the line at the cash register. My dad's hand shook a little as he took the familiar tan ready-roll package from his shirt pocket and lit up another Camel cigarette. He inhaled and blew out the smoke, coughed, and inhaled again. He looked a little rough, and I figured that he was needing a drink. He usually kept a pint of Echo Springs stashed under the driver's seat of his truck.

"Gonna mosey over to the domino parlor and see if'n I can't win a nickel or two," he said. That beery, smoky place in the basement of the bank building was his hangout, shoot the moon, his game.

We paid, and the four of us split up. I walked alone a block east to the wagon yard where I'd parked my cattle truck. There, winding my way through the gravel lot, crowded with horses and wagons, trucks, and pickups, parked every which way, I spotted old man Nahnahpwa and his wife, Lucy, and another Comanche couple eating their noon meal on a blue-and-white-striped cotton blanket that was spread on the ground on the east side of their wagon. The old lady saw me and waved. I veered off toward them. Away from the blanket, a blackened coffeepot perked on a small iron grill resting over a bed of red coals.

The old man's team of two sleek brown mules had been unhooked, and they stood in harness on the west side of the wagon, trace chains looped up over the hames. Together with three saddle horses tied with them, the mules munched on a bale of millet hay that had been busted for them on the bare ground.

Lucy, still in her parade buckskin and her gray hair in long braids, got up from the blanket as I approached and came toward me and put out her hand. "*Mahtsai*," she said in Comanche—literally, get ahold of it. We shook hands. Then, in Indian-accented English, she said, "Okie, have something to eat." She motioned me closer toward the seated blanket group.

I stepped over and extended my hand to old man Nahnahpwa. "Keep your seat," I said.

"Hah, mahduahwe," the old man said. He turned to hold up a rough-used hand toward me, causing his dangling peyote-bird earrings to shake as he did so.

"Tsa nuh nuisikite uh puhneets," I said, taking his hand. It makes me feel good to see you. I used the Comanche I'd picked up as a kid. It pleased him. Several of us Vernon High School boxers had trained in old man Nahnahpwa's barn, and I'd stayed over lots of nights with his son, Marvin, who'd been my good friend.

"Hah!" the old man said, nodding in greeting.

I moved closer and bent down to shake hands with the other couple on the blanket. "How are you, Frank, Ida?" I said. I knew them. Frank was the old man's cousin, and Ida, Frank's wife. Like old man Nahnahpwa and Lucy, they were still in the traditional Comanche clothes they'd worn for the parade, their hair in braids. The two men had tan-cotton blankets draped over their shoulders, the two women, fringed red-and-white shawls.

I squatted in the dirt, just off the blanket. Still standing, Lucy bent over and picked up a wooden platter of grilled slices of beef and extended it toward me. "Have something to eat," she said.

"Already ate, but thanks," I said, though the meat smelled good. "Wouldn't mind having some of that coffee. Any left?"

She leaned over and picked up a tin cup from the blanket and shook out some remaining drops on the ground behind her. Then, using a folded-over white cup towel to protect her hand, she lifted the coffeepot from the grill and poured the cup full of steaming black coffee. After handing me the hot cup, she set the pot back down on the grill and found her place again on the blanket, next to the old man.

"We heard you were back," she said. "Old man's been wantin' to see you. Been needin' us a lawyer."

"Hah," old man Nahnahpwa said, nodding in agreement with his wife. Then he said something more in Comanche, but I was only able to catch the phrase, *"puhiwi taibo"*—banker.

"That banker," Lucy translated, "let mud run into our pond. Just about ruined it."

"Son of a bitch!" the old man said. I already knew from high-school days that he could cuss in English. Then he switched back to Comanche to add some other words with equal vehemence.

"Old man says they left the gate down several times, and the cows got out, and he had to go look for 'em," Lucy said.

"You mean Traynor?" I asked.

"Hah!" Nahnahpwa said in confirmation.

"Came out with them big trucks and drilling rig," Lucy said. "Looked for oil. Just about ruined our pond. Old man wants you to make 'em clean it up or sue in court."

I knew the pond. It was a deep hole of blue, spring-fed water, in the middle of the pasture east of Lucy and Nahnahpwa's house, down toward the creek. I myself had learned to swim in it, with their son, Marvin, and a lot of other boys our age.

"I'm not a lawyer, though," I said. "Had to quit law school. But I can talk with Traynor if you want me to."

"We'd be much obliged, Okie," Lucy said.

I finished my coffee and set the cup back on the blanket. "Gotta get on down to the schoolhouse for the program," I said. I stood up.

"We gotta go, too," Lucy said. The whole bunch started getting up. Frank gave the old man a hand. I shook hands with the old lady, then with Frank and Ida. Old man Nahnahpwa adjusted the tan-cotton blanket over his left shoulder and gathered it under his right arm with the opposite hand. He put out his right, and I took it.

"It's good to see you," I said in English. "It makes me think of that young man, my friend, that used to live in your house." Out of respect for people's feelings, Comanches never mentioned the name of a person who'd died.

"*Hah*," the old man said. His sunken eyes, plucked clean of eyebrows or eyelashes, teared up a little. He let go my hand, then, and drew an eagle-feather peyote fan with a beaded buckskin handle from a fold of his blanket. He guided me over to the smoldering coals of the fire and stationed me beside it. Then he opened a little leather bag at his waist and took out three or four small cedar or juniper branches and dropped them on the hot coals.

Pungent smoke quickly curled up from the fire. The old man caught the smoke with his fan and drew it over to me and wafted it all around my body and up to my face. All the while, he murmured some low words in Comanche. I could not understand the words, but I knew that he was giving me a blessing.

When he was finished, I thanked him and shook his hand. I felt good as I headed off.

FOUR

I climbed into my old cattle truck, fired it up, and nosed onto the street. I doubled back a block and drove three blocks south on Main toward the school. But I might as well have walked there from town because the attendance was so great that I had to circle once and then park a block and a half away.

I didn't go into the auditorium directly. Instead, I went over to the southside front doors of the adjoining old main building. Buff brick and three stories plus a basement, it was nearly as old as the town, while the auditorium was a one-story, more recent afterthought on the main building's west side. Fixed to the back side of the main building, snaking down from the top floor to the ground, was a steel tubular fire-escape slide, big enough for bent-over kids to walk up through. It had been a great place to play, after hours and on weekends, when I was a boy.

I mounted the front steps of the old main school building, pulled open a heavy, squeaking door, and went in. Dim electric lights shone in the wide hallway. I turned left and walked slowly along the oiled-wood floor.

I scanned the framed class pictures that hung on the yellow, plastered north wall, to the right of the door to the principal's office. And I soon found the picture I was looking for—a photograph of the Vernon High graduating class of 1930. Dub Ready and I had been inseparable in school, and there he was, standing to my left in the group picture. Dub had had to take the third grade twice. So, despite the fact that he was a year older, he'd wound up in the same class, all the way through school, with his sister, Juanita, and me.

Separately inset into the two lower corners of the black-and-white 1930 class photograph were two close-up oval shots, one of me, as class president, the other of Juanita, as that year's Turkey Queen. I studied her face. A couple of nights earlier, I'd gone to the picture show with a married cousin to see the new Walt Disney cartoon-movie, *Snow White and the Seven Dwarfs*, and, in that picture on the school wall, it seemed to me that that's who Juanita looked like, Snow White.

I stepped across the hallway, then, to the cotton-bale-sized glass case squatting against the south wall, opposite the principal's office. Tacked on that wall above the case was a blue-and-white silk banner with the appliquéd words, "Blue Devils," scrawled across a grinning Satan's horned face. On tiered shelves inside the display case were each year's formal group pictures of Vernon's athletic teams, together with the trophies and awards they'd won.

I bent over to get a better look at the photograph, on the second shelf, of the 1930 Vernon High football team. There we were, wearing our leather helmets and lightly padded uniforms, all staring seriously into the camera, looking as fierce as we had been able to manage. The first row of players sat cross-legged on grass, the second knelt behind them, and the third row stood in back. Dub Ready, the team captain, was in the front rank, with me on his right. He was holding the silver trophy we'd won as that year's Southern Six champions. Dub had been a tackle, I a tailback on offense, safety on defense. In games, he'd always tried to make me look good.

I straightened up, turned away from the case, and headed west in the hallway to a steep interior flight of concrete stairs leading down into the crowd-jammed old barny and rectangular room that doubled as Vernon's assembly hall and basketball court. Banks of fixed seats on each side of the court were packed with people. So were rows of metal folding chairs that had been set up on the hardwood floor.

The gym's plastered ceiling, with its twin rows of electric lights, was really too low for basketball. If you put great arch on a ball, you could literally shoot the lights out. That actually happened once, at least to one of those ceiling lights, in a Vernon-Devol county tournament game I played in.

Dub saw me as soon as I came down the stairs. He left the small party of men he'd been talking with and came over. He shook hands with me vigorously and drew me slightly aside.

"Long time no see, Okie," he said.

"Who writes your lines?" I said.

"Been a while."

"Maybe longer," I said.

"Missed seein' ya."

"Me, too," I said.

"My old man was mad at you, back then, but I never was," he said. "Shit, he was always mad at ever'body. You know, hell, Juanita and I run off and moved to town."

"Glad to see you again, Dub," I said.

During our senior year in high school, Dub and Juanita had moved into Vernon and rented an apart-

ment together on the second floor of the old post-
office building, across from the school. They'd said
that they had to do that to graduate. Essaquahnahdale School, out in the country near where they
lived, only went to the eighth grade, and when it
rained, the roads from their house into Vernon could
get impassable. But everyone also knew that Dub
and Juanita had been glad to get away from home,
too, back then, for whatever reason.

"Juanita's not mad, either," Dub said. "She had a
little run a bad luck, afterwards, a course, but she's
back home, now, and doin' okay."

"Glad to hear it," I said.

"Listen, Rough, I'm on a deal you might could
hep me with," Dub said in a lower voice. He used an
old nickname. We once called ourselves Rough and
Ready. The R bar R was what we'd said we'd name
the ranch that we talked about someday owning
together. "You still close to old man Nahnahpwa and
them Indians, ain'tcha?"

"Hope so. But I've been gone, you know."

"Well, I run onto some strictly confidential information about a new oil pool, and I already spent a
heap of good money to block up leases on several
sections in that area, southeast of town," Dub said.
"But I need the section and a half that old man
Nahnahpwa and his kinfolks own. You could talk
him into signin' and make yourself a little override
percentage in the bargain. Whadda ya say, Okie? You
wanna get in on it?"

"The last time you talked me into a deal," I said,
"hauling off a load of copper tubes and brass fittings
from that old abandoned refinery at night and selling it at Wichita Falls, we almost got caught and sent
to the pen." I was grinning.

Just then, a student bugler began blowing a shaky
assembly.

"This ain't like that," Dub said, serious, leaning in to me. "Go with me Saturday mornin' on the rabbit drive, down at 'Squahnahdale, and we'll talk it over some more. I'll come git ya, out at the Billings place, at nine. Okay?"

"I think I can work it into my busy schedule," I said.

"Bring Hudge's four-ten; they don't allow no twenty-twos," he said.

"No shit?" I said.

"You still a tough little bastard," Dub said.

"Little?" I said.

We shook hands once more, quietly said again that it was good to see each other, and headed to our seats. Dub went up front to join his sister, Juanita, and his wife, Audrey, extending a quick hand and a hushed greeting to two or three men seated with their families along the way. I found a vacant folding chair near the back, next to a farmer from Lincoln Valley, Gar Malcolm, who I'd recently bought some cattle from.

The flags were marched in by two Boy Scouts and set in their places on either side of the stage. We all stood up and gave the pledge of allegiance in unison and in the usual way, right hands, palms up, pointed toward the American flag.

As we sat back down afterward, squat and chalky-faced Judge Jesse Dowlin, wearing a greenish three-piece suit and his usual tan-blond wig that my dad always rightly said looked like a possum hide, stepped to the lectern. He was the master of ceremonies, of course.

"My friends," Judge Dowlin began solemnly, his orator's voice carrying throughout the auditorium, "no Armistice Day should pass without fitting tribute to our native sons, who some twenty years ago marched forth to World War battlefields, some never to return."

Ten minutes later, a pretty short time for the judge, he closed out his introductory words. "A few scattered doughboys determined to win twenty years ago would have accomplished little," he said. "But hundreds of thousands of doughboys, all of one mind and with a will to win, brought quick and positive victory. So it is today in our national war upon poverty, want, and depression. We carry on. The spirit of America still lives!"

When the applause had died down, Judge Dowlin, whose forced good cheer, I thought, had to be pretty close to a service-connected disability, led the crowd in singing: "Over There," "Those Caissons Go Rolling Along," and "It's a Long Way to Tipperary." We didn't need songbooks.

Old man Nahnahpwa and his wife, Lucy, got first and second prize for the best-dressed Indians, though they weren't present to pick up their ribbons. Wardell and Ahpeatone came in first and second for the best school floats. A Vernon senior girl, Ida Faye Hunt, was crowned Turkey Queen. Two high-school boys gave original orations. One was "President Wilson's War Message" by Billy McBride, the other "Armistice Day Ideals" by John Phil Grady. Brother George Tanner of the First Baptist Church delivered the benediction.

Afterward, I waited out on the playground by the swings, visiting and shaking hands as people left. I wanted to see Juanita.

Dub and Audrey came out before she did. Dub and I shook hands and agreed again on the Saturday rabbit drive. Audrey and I hugged enthusiastically. She was the kind of person that you were always glad to run into. She made you feel good.

"Gee, Okie, we've been wantin' to see you," Audrey said, when we'd stepped apart. Her short, brown hair clung to her head in tight waves, and she was as tiny as ever, still only coming up to my shoulders, even in the gray-suede, high-heeled pumps she wore with a neat dark blue wool tailored suit and a pale blue, silk, high-collared blouse. Incongruously, a black-and-red-carpetbag briefcase hung on a wide strap over her right shoulder.

"Bring your sewing kit?" I nodded toward the bag.

"My doctor bag," Audrey said. "Well, my nurse bag, more like it. I'm a nurse at the Vernon Hospital. But I take the bag with me everywhere. People always approach me for help, like I was a doctor."

I wasn't surprised. Audrey'd always seemed to me like a Florence Nightingale type—although she was certainly spunkier and feistier than Florence would have been, a nurse more like Ann Sheridan could have played.

"Glad to be back in good old Vernon?" she asked.

"Something like being dropped down in Oz, to tell the truth, after all the places I've been," I said. "Lots of changes, and I feel a little like a stranger, here."

"Home to stay?"

"How're you going to keep 'em down on the farm, after they've seen the *farm*?" I said.

A grade behind us at Vernon High School, Audrey had been Dub's steady girlfriend our last two years there. Those two and Juanita and I had double-dated a lot and done practically everything else together, too—picture shows, pie suppers, dances, horse rides, and even early-morning squirrel hunting.

"I hope you'll come see us, Okie," Audrey said.

"A free meal'd be a big draw," I replied.

"Come anytime, and you don't need a meal ticket," Audrey said. "I mean it."

She joined Dub, who'd been shaking hands around and politicking, and they left.

Juanita saw me right away when she emerged from the auditorium. But she took her time coming over. She first picked up a friend's little three-year-old daughter, a child very cutely dressed in white patent-leather shoes and a red-velvet dress that had a tiny white-lace apron over it. The little girl's hair was done up in long Shirley Temple curls.

Juanita bounced her and whirled her around. The child laughed out loud. Juanita grinned broadly, enjoying herself. She'd always been crazy about kids, and she was great with them. She'd taken care of people's kids during our senior year, and not just to make spending money. She'd really loved doing it.

Juanita finally gave the little girl a last hug, kissed her on the cheek, and put her down. She said goodbye to the mother and some others standing nearby, then walked slowly on over to the swings where I was.

"You planning on helping assassinate the rabbits, down at Essaquahnahdale?" I asked, after we'd said hello. It might have seemed like a strange question, because you didn't usually find women hunters at rabbit drives. But Juanita wasn't the usual woman. Audrey either, for that matter.

"You going?" she answered with a question.

She looked just the same, except that her face was slightly more angular than it had been a few years earlier, and that made her more attractive. Her long and curly black hair contrasted stunningly with the almost translucent white skin of her face, still unblemished except for the black beauty mark that had always been there, just above the right corner of her red mouth. Tall, lean, small-breasted, she could have easily been a Montgomery Ward catalogue model, I thought, in the knit-wool green dress she wore, which matched the color of her eyes and stylishly came down to mid-calf.

"Told your Tom Mix brother I would," I said.

A lightbulb could have run a month on the current that charged the air between Juanita and me. I wondered if people were looking at us.

"Audrey's going with Dub," she said. "But I just thought I'd go and do women's work—help the community ladies set up coffee and doughnuts at the start. I feel like I still live down there—I'm a member of their farmers' community association— even though the old house's gone. But I can't stay. I've got to go to Cookietown to see a guy about a load of alfalfa. You want to go riding next Wednesday?"

"Be better than a kick in the head," I said. I shut off a grin before it could get started good. I didn't want to act like I'd come down with what my dad would have called a bad case of the eagers.

"Probably see you Saturday, then, for a minute— and next week," she said.

She smiled. I felt a little woozy, like I used to as a kid after guzzling a quick couple of 3.2 beers on an empty stomach. God, what a hold she still had on me!

We shook hands then, sort of formally, and each turned away, to go in search of our vehicles.

FIVE

Saturday morning at six, my dad and I were sitting in his old gourd green Ford half-ton truck in front of the Truckers Cafe. That tiny eatery was like a little toe at the foot of the hill on the north end of Vernon's Main Street. My dad and I were getting tired of our own cooking.

When we saw the full-bodied proprietress on the inside, coming toward the front, we got out and waited for her to unlock.

"How you boys doin'?" she said, and held the door open for us. This was the thirties, but her hairstyle was stuck in the twenties—short, hennaed, and tightly marcelled. The little wooden tag pinned to a bulging breast pocket looked like it had been made by some kid in daily vacation Bible school. The tag said, "Irma." That was old news to my dad and me.

"Walk this way, Okie," my dad said, cackling a little to himself over this regular joke. He limped out ahead toward the nearest table, bobbing up and down in well-worn cowboy boots. The "jake leg" was what he called his affliction, caused, he said, by

drinking bad whiskey when he was a boy in
Mississippi, though I thought it might actually have
resulted from infantile paralysis. My dad's usual
joke got the reaction he wanted from Irma.

"Hudge, I swan, you're a real mess!" she said, and
snickered like a Shetland. She pushed the door
behind us and headed back toward the shiny coffee
urn. Irma was big. Her blue-taffeta waitress uniform
bulged at the waist, and she bounced in a good many
places, front and back, as she walked.

My dad and I scraped out metal chairs and sat
down at a white, porcelain-topped table. Irma
trucked over right away with two white mugs,
steam rising from them. She set the coffee in front of
us, then straightened up and waited for everything
in her uniform to settle back into place. Irma'd over-
done the white face powder, and one of the two thin
maroon lines she'd penciled in where her eyebrows
should have been was noticeably higher than the
other. It struck me that she looked like a female foil
in an old Buster Keaton silent movie. It also struck
me that she probably needed to get a brighter lightbulb and a better mirror in her bathroom.

"Anything hot?" my dad said, cocking a rake's
eye at Irma from under his sweat-stained narrow-
brim Stetson. There was a kind of conspiratorial grin
on his face, which was permanently reddened by a
million tiny burst capillaries.

"Just me and the java, hon," she said, and winked
at him.

Lord have mercy! I thought. My dad was running
around with old Irma? She was nine or ten years
younger than he was and at least four or five inches
taller. Even if he was standing on his left leg, the
straight one.

In fact, Irma was as big as Kate Smith and nearly

as tall as me. She outweighed either one of us. My dad was a bantamweight, maybe 126 pounds. With his boots on.

Irma, I imagined, would probably go as a light-heavy. Dripping wet—a scary thought.

Irma caught me sizing her up. "You dad says you done give up bein' a *lie-yer*, Okie," she said, poking me with both her remark and her elbow at the same time.

"Had to," I said. "Run out of money the start of my third year in law school." My dad knew better, but I didn't figure Irma needed to. I'd found myself now and then talking again in a southwest Oklahoma way, even though I'd not been back home in Vernon for even a month.

"Vernon got enough lawyers, anyhow," Irma said. She was probably right, I thought. There were four, and that was one lawyer for nearly every four hundred men, women, and children in the town. "You bachin' with Hudge, now, out the old Billings place, and tradin' cattle to make a living, like him," Irma said. It was a statement of fact.

"Case of groundhog," I said. "Climb a tree or get eat by the dogs."

"Seen you old sweetheart since coming home?" Irma asked. She was punching me again. "Reckon Juanita Ready's been back two years, ain't that about right, Hudge?"

"Hit weren't no gain for Cash County, you ask me," my dad said.

"Run into her Armistice Day." I said this calmly, although my stomach felt like it had turned over at the mention of her name. "Probably see her at the Essaquahnahdale rabbit drive today. Her brother Dub's gonna come by and get me."

"The high sheriff," my dad said, a tone of some derision in his voice. "Air one of 'em, him and

Juanita, bound to git a feller in trouble. Ortn't to get mixed up with 'em no more."

"Don't aim to," I said. Back to lying again.

"Terrible thing 'bout their folks, 'bout the Readys, burnin' theyselves up, wadn't it?" Irma said. "And dern strange, too."

"Only got coffee and conversation, here, or could a person order somethin' to eat?" I said. I grinned quickly, but the words still sounded harsher than I'd meant them to.

Irma's face reddened through the powder. Which wasn't easy. She curtly took our order without saying anything further. Biscuits and gravy, slab bacon, and two eggs each, sunny-side up. She knew to bring my dad some Tabasco sauce for his eggs, without his saying so.

We were still the only customers in the place. It was early. Also, the Depression was continuing, and most people couldn't afford to eat in a café. Hell, I thought, we couldn't either, for that matter. The food came fast.

The weekly *Vernon Herald* was out. "A Blue Ribbon Newspaper Serving a Community of Diversified Production," it claimed, right under the masthead. I went over to the cash register and picked up copies for both of us and left a nickel. I figured we'd put one of them back, later. My dad and I read the local news as we ate.

"Ten carloads of dressed turkeys done shipped this fall by Cash County Produce," my dad read from a front-page article, his horned-rim drugstore glasses low on his nose. "Says '37 the best year'n the last ten. Says they havin' trouble gittin' pickers. Hit ain't no damn wonder! Sonsabitches still payin' the same three cents a head you pore old mama got when *she* picked turkeys fer 'em."

He pulled a Camel package from his gray work-shirt pocket, shook out a cigarette, and tamped it on the tabletop. He stretched out his left boot to fish a kitchen match from the front pocket of his faded tight Levi's and struck it on the bottom of his chair. He lit up and took a long drag.

I'd never used cigarettes. They hurt your wind. But I'd always liked the smell of my dad's Camel smoke when I was a kid, riding with him in his truck. There had always been something manly and tough about that scent for me. Still was. And I'd felt the same way, too—and this was crazier—about my dad's special sweaty smell when he hadn't masked it with shaving lotion.

Dad exhaled, then hacked and coughed, something that had been happening more and more. I worked at taking no notice. He took a sip of coffee and got control, finally, ate a strip of bacon with his fingers, then went back to reading, moving his lips silently as his eyes went back and forth across the page.

"They raised the number of Cash County men in the WPA to six hundred," I said.

"We Piddle Around," my dad said, idly.

"They gravel streets and build roads and schools, built a big part of Kraker Park, down on the creek," I countered. My dad didn't respond, and I went on reading. "Fewer foreclosures this year than in '36, wage income up a little."

"When Roosevelt took his seat, we commenced to climb, and we clumb!" my dad said.

We had, indeed, I thought. But it'd been a slow climb. Too many kids still got little more than corn bread and beans at home and managed to make it only because of the hot-lunch program at school. And a lot of people, those that hadn't gone off to California, were only able to hold body and soul together, and that barely, because of the highway work or sewing-room jobs that they got from the Works Progress Administration.

Then I noticed a curious little story, tucked away on the second page. "Listen to this," I said. I started reading aloud:

"Douglas 'Poss' Tatums, thirty-two-year-old Wardell Negro, was arrested Tuesday night by Sheriff J.W. Ready and Deputy Gordon Merkle at an upstairs room of the New Wardell Hotel for the detestable crime against nature.

"Long suspected by the officers of this practice, the Negro pervert and a white Vernon businessman were followed as they left the Negro's beer parlor in Wardell and were detained soon after the Vernon man obtained a key and the two men entered the hotel room."

My dad interrupted. "The man from Vernon, who was it?" he asked, rustling through his own copy of the paper to find the story for himself.

"Yeah, that's just the point," I said. "They don't say. And listen to the rest:

"Tatums is being held in the county jail, pending formal charges. The white businessman was not identified, and charges have yet to be filed against him."

"Sure, old Poss Tatums runs gamblin' and two or three colored ho's out'n the back room a that beer joint a hisn," my dad said. "But he ain't a bad guy, and I never heard nobody say he was queer." He found the story, then, and began to read it for himself.

Unlike Vernon, where Negroes had never been allowed to live, the town of Wardell, eleven miles southeast, counted a Negro population of around two hundred. They were segregated on Wardell's east side.

"Maybe he's not," I said. "And, besides, what

about the Vernon guy? Why don't they tell who *he* was and bring charges against *him*?"

"He more'n likely worked sump'n out with your friend J.W.," my dad said. "You might ask him on the way to the rabbit drive." He looked up from his paper and stared at me for a full second.

We finished breakfast without any more discussion of the news. Then we loaded up again in my dad's old truck and drove back out to the Billings place.

SIX

I milked the Jersey cow we kept in the corrugated-metal barn in back, then slopped my dad's two white Poland China meat hogs. He put out some cottonseed cake for the motley-faced black steer he was also fattening out, then hayed and pumped some water for his horse and mine. His was a big, half-thoroughbred sorrel gelding called Barney, with white stocking feet; mine, a young little ashy quarter horse stud. I called him Badger.

I brought in a five-gallon can of coal oil and filled the cookstove tank and the glass lamps, while my dad carried in two buckets of fresh water at a time, one in each hand, from the outside pump.

"When old lady Hungerford comes to clean next week, we gotta get her to trim them wicks and wipe the sut out'n them lamp chimbleys, too," my dad said. He was breathing heavily from carrying the water. "Hain't got the wind I used to," he said. "Least dab a work, and I'm might neart as weak as cat piss."

I said, "You gittin' old, I guess, Daddy." I said this even though I knew he would only be forty-five in

January. Around him, I sometimes talked the way I
had as a kid. And I often felt a little like a kid, too,
when I was with him. It worried me to see him fail-
ing some.

I brought in an armload of oak firewood and some
kindling he'd chopped for the potbellied stove in the
dining room.

The white clapboard Billings place that my dad
rented was just outside the Vernon city limits, on the
east side. It was four rooms and a kitchen on the
back, and it had none of the conveniences that the
majority of the houses in town did—no electricity,
running water, gas, indoor toilet, or telephone. There
was a twenty-acre pasture with the Billings place,
plus a large plot where my dad put in a big vegetable
garden every spring.

Dub Ready showed up promptly at nine o'clock,
just like he'd said he would. He idled into our dirt
driveway in a nearly new, streamlined, blue, 1936
Ford V-Eight four-door sedan. It had a magnified
sheriff's badge stenciled in white on each of the front
doors.

My dad and I heard him pull in, and we both
stepped out onto the porch. Dad's old muckledy-
dun dog ran to the car and began to snarl and bark.

"Step down, J.W.," my dad called. And then he
growled to the dog in a low voice, "Git out from
heah, suh!" The dog stopped barking at once and
slunk back, eyes down. My dad had a command
over animals that was a near marvel.

"Nawsir, Mr. Dunn, thank you just the same," Dub
said through the rolled-down window. "Guess we'll
head on. You goin' too, ain'tcha?"

"Be along dreckly," my dad said. "Stud Wampler
gon' come by an carry me." I knew that my dad had
tried to get Marsh Traynor to go, too, but the burly
banker had declined, saying that he'd probably go

hunting, instead. My dad and I figured that the real reason was Dub, or, as my dad put it, "Marsh didn't want no part of nothin' that had Dub Ready in it."

As I went around to the other side of the Ford, my dad asked, "Gotcha cotridges, son?"

I held up my left hand to show him the yellow-and-black cardboard box of shells I carried. I opened the back door on my side and laid the 410 alongside Dub's gun in the rear seat, then climbed into the front with him. I was taking my dad's double-barreled 410-gauge shotgun, leaving him to use his other gun, a single-shot 20-gauge.

"How you like my car?" Dub asked me. He put it in gear, nodded to Dad, and we started off. "Got it new for six hundred dollars from Strickland Ford. Leasin' it to the county for more'n enough to make the payments."

"Good deal," I said. Most people in Vernon who owned cars still drove model-A Fords, or old-model Chevys that were just about as square and chunky. A goodly number of aged model-T Fords were still on the roads, too. None of the older cars, of course, could match the sleek, swept-back look of the Ford V-Eight and its boat-prow radiator grill. Even the sound of the older cars' horns seemed outdated, compared to the newer Fords, say. Old horns said a groaning oo-gah; the new ones, a long, sharp beep.

"Audrey couldn't come, after all; helping with a baby," Dub said. "Smart, bringin' you coat. Looks like it's comin' up a norther."

I was wearing a red mackinaw over a black-wool shirt and tan khakis, an old pair of work shoes, and a brown-wool, billed cap with earflaps that I could turn down if I needed to. I was also wearing long-handles under my clothes.

The November sky was overcast, with a cranky, darkening blue bank in the northwest, and the eternal wind of southwest Oklahoma had shifted around to the north and picked up some. The temperature was dropping, too.

Dub was a lot more dressed up than I was. Black cowboy hat, nearly new brown-rawhide boots, nice short brown-leather jacket over a gray-and-black plaid shirt, and black-wool pants. His sheriff's badge was pinned to the left pocket flap of his jacket, and he wore his gun belt and holstered Colt revolver under the jacket.

"Y'all lived in that same Billings place once before," Dub said.

"The hog returns to his wallow and the dog to his vomit," I said. We got to the McAlesters' corner and jogged left. We would go down to South Boundary Street, take it west seven or eight blocks across the tracks through what people called Snuff Ridge to the gravel Wardell highway, then head south. Dub unwrapped a big Roitan cigar that he took from the inside pocket of his jacket and lit it with a book match. Smoke curled around his face.

I went on. "We left the Billings place my junior year and moved over to that southside house on Virginia, you remember, the only house my dad ever owned. And he bought that model-A Ford car, then, too, the only car he ever owned."

"A good old car, tied ever bundle," Dub said. "Double-dated a lot in that old thang."

"My dad never said, of course, but I'm pretty sure he bought both the house and the car on account of me," I continued. "When we lived in the Billings place, before, I always had to walk to town, and my sister, Alene, had the only other bedroom besides my folks' room; I slept on the divan in the living room. My dad was hubbin' it pretty close in '29, but I think he just about strained his milk to make things good for me, my last two years in high school."

"You and Hudge was always close," Dub said.

"Never showed it," I said.

"Better'n me and my old man; we wasn't close, and he showed it all the time," Dub said. "Scars to prove it." He laughed a kind of false laugh.

"He beat y'all up?" I asked. "I always wondered."

"That ain't the worst kind of scars," Dub said. He quickly changed the subject, then. "Alene still out in Long Beach?" he asked.

My sister, who was two years older than me, had graduated from Vernon High School two years ahead of me and Dub. She and the local guy she married, Jake Lewis, moved to Long Beach right after they'd graduated. He'd landed a job in the oil fields there.

Alene and I had been close, like Dub and Juanita. And my sister and I were about as curiously different in appearance, too, as those two were. Dub's hair was red, Juanita's black. My sister Alene was fair, like our dad; I was dark like our mother, always looking like I had a suntan, even when I didn't.

Alene used to tease me and say that I was adopted, or found. Remembering that made me think about a time when I was in grade school and went down to the street corner in front of Herschel Brothers Drugstore to see if my dad would give me a nickel for candy. A cattle auctioneer who didn't normally hang out there with the cow traders said to my dad: "He you boy, Hudge?"

"That's what my old lady tells me," my dad said. I knew it was a joke, of course. Everybody had laughed but me.

As we turned west on South Boundary, I said to Dub, "Jake's pumping for Standard Oil out in Long Beach. That's who he got me a job roughnecking for, when I left out of here after we graduated. Worked

six months there, then went to prizefighting down
through Mexico for another six before I came back to
school at Cameron College and up at Norman."

"You mama never got over that stroke, did she?"
Dub said.

"She never did," I said. "And, poor old thing, she
lingered on for another two weeks after Dad took
her home from the hospital, never quite right. She
couldn't move her left side, and she couldn't talk.
She'd look at you like she was kind of scared and
mad at the same time and hold on to your hand real
tight. It was a blessing when another stroke hit her.
We buried her on the coldest damned day of that
winter." My voice caught, and I turned away for a
moment and looked out the window.

"At least, my own folks didn't linger," Dub said,
matter-of-factly.

"They set fire to the house, then killed themselves, I heard," I said. Dub clinched his jaw and
said nothing. "I was really sorry to hear it," I added.
Neither one of us spoke for a while.

About a third of the gently rolling land we were
driving through had never been broken out and was
still in native grasses. Here and there in these dry fall
gray pastures, behind the barbed-wire fences, we
could see scattered clusters of mixed-breed cattle
that had quit looking for grazing and had begun to
drift south, rumps to the increasingly colder wind
that blew out of the north.

Half the farmed land on each side of the road had
been sown in wheat the past September, and the
young shoots in the drill rows looked like close-set
lines of green hog bristles in giant hairbrushes.
Other fields were white with rows of cotton almost
ready to pull. It was pretty scraggly cotton, though,
because of the drought that had hit the county in the
last half of the year.

"You keep the old home place?" I asked, finally. We started up Finchum's Hill. I remembered that gravel incline as a hard pull for a loaded wagon and team—and not easy for a model-T, or even a model-A. The Ford V-Eight took it without a complaint.

"Naw," Dub said. "Juanita made me sell Mama and Daddy's place. She come back from St. Louis in poor health and head over heels in debt. She married there, you know."

"I heard," I said.

"Twice."

"Twice?" I said. I didn't know that.

"Twice," Dub said. "Both the sonsabitches no 'count. First one bad as the second, and that one turned out a dope fiend. Dad helped her, and she borrowed a lot of money to go into some wild oil scheme with her second husband. Chickenshit stole her blind and then took off. She limped back here to Vernon."

"The baby?" I made myself ask. I didn't look at him.

"Put up for adoption, I reckon, by the Methodist home that the old man made her go to."

"We wanted to marry, you know," I said. "But she wouldn't go up against your dad."

"He was crazy mad—maybe just crazy. Juanita never forgive him—for a lot a things. Married both times, I think, just to spite *him*, much as anything else."

"I've been pretty down on myself about it," I said. "I should have made her marry me, whether your dad liked it or not, instead of my just taking off for Long Beach and Mexico."

"Not anybody can make Juanita do what she don't wanna do; you know that," Dub said.

"What kind of dope was he on, her last husband," I asked after a time. "Marijuana?"

"Yeah, that, for sure—but worse," Dub said. "Morphine, she told me."

We passed rural Soldier Valley School on our right, a one-story redbrick building with a tin roof. "Women gonna spread dinner there, for us, after we done huntin'," Dub said.

"How's Juanita doing since she got back?" I asked.

"Had a lot of health problems, herself—female trouble, I think. Old Doc Watson's treatin' her."

"My dad says he wouldn't let that sonofabitch work on one of his calves," I said.

"'Bout right, too," Dub said. "And Juanita's still borrowed to the hilt. She's been leasin' our old home place, runnin' a few head of cattle. She's got a crop of cotton on it. But, hell, you ain't gonna make nothin' on a upland farm, not this year, not with this kind a drought. Looks to me like she's about ready to go under again."

"Too bad," I said, and I meant it. "Talking about her husband's oil schemes, what kind of an oil scheme are you trying to get me in?"

"Marsh Traynor hates my guts, you know, the same as he hated my dad," Dub said. "Long time ago, my dad foreclosed on Traynor's dad and once tried to foreclose on Traynor, too. I arrested him one time for selling whiskey. Traynor'd cut his wrists before he'd let me in on anything good. But I found it out, anyway, last Monday. Found out they done drilled a test well on old man Nahnahpwa's home quarter, in the bottom on this side of East Cash Creek. Hit a big strike at about thirty-five hundred feet, and then plugged it, 'til they could, quick, block up a bunch of leases."

"Who told you that?" I asked.

"Got drunk with that kid, Jonesy, that works for

Traynor," Dub said. "He let it slip. I wasn't as drunk as I let on, and I got in gear right quick. Laid out a right smart a money, and I've awready blocked up leases ever which a way on this side of East Cash, except for old man Nahnahpwa's six quarters along the creek. That's what I need you for. The old man won't sign a lease with me. I think Traynor let a lot of muddy water run into one of his ponds, and he's mad about it."

"Yeah, the old man told me," I said. "But you can't get an oil lease on Indian land unless the Bureau of Indian Affairs in Anadarko okays it."

"I can git that done, don't sweat it," Dub said. "What I need is the old man and his wife's John Henrys. I awready got enough leases to get well. But *their* section and a half'd be the icin'. Juanita's achin' to get in on it, needin' money bad, but, hell, I told her I never took her to raise. You, though, Okie, I'll let you have a one-cent override on them Indian leases, if you git 'em for me. Deal?"

"Well, maybe I can talk with old man Nahnah-pwa," I said. I could sure use a little oil money, I thought. And it wasn't as if the old Indian wouldn't make plenty, too.

"Good," Dub said. "Get with it, though, before old Traynor does."

That raised a puzzling question in my mind. If this was such a hot oil find, why hadn't Traynor himself blocked up leases on all the land around old man Nahnahpwa's? But I didn't raise that question. I don't know why.

We were about a mile from the Essaquahnahdale curve when we came on to the dead coyotes. For a stretch of about fifty yards on the west side of the road, to our right, there were about a dozen and a half carcasses, hanging head down like sad trophies from the *bois d'arc* posts that, at regular intervals, held up the four-strand barbed-wire fence along there.

"Farmers' association been strychnine-baitin' coyotes a lot around here," Dub said. "Puts 'em in convulsions, and they kick off quick."

"Tough way to die," I said.

"Ain't no easy ways, I reckon," Dub said.

"No wonder they've got jackrabbit problems," I said. "Killing all the coyotes."

I rolled down my window a little. Dub's cigar smoke was getting to me. A state highway sign on my side of the road read: "Wardell—6 miles." Wardell reminded me of the curious story I'd read in the *Vernon Herald*.

"What's the deal about Poss Tatums, down at Wardell, and what the *Herald* called a 'detestable crime against nature'?" I asked. "Who's the white Vernon businessman, and how come just Tatums is in jail?"

"Hey, don't worry about none a that," Dub said, dismissively. "We ain't even gonna charge old Poss, anyhow."

He obviously didn't want to talk about it, and I let it drop, like he said.

Up a slight incline, we came to the curve to the left in the main road that led toward Wardell. Off about fifty yards to our right was the shingle-roofed, limestone-block Essaquahnahdale School building. Dub turned that way, onto the dirt road that ran west in front of the school, and then, pretty soon, right again into the driveway.

"Dang good turnout for the rabbit drive," he said.

We pulled in among the nearly forty or so pickups and cars already parked every which way on the large gravel playground at the west side of the building. Near the back door of the school, on the north side, the community women had already set up two long, makeshift tables of sawhorses and planks and covered them with overlapping white tablecloths.

On one of the tables, there were three great steaming, blue-enamel coffeepots, brought out from the school kitchen, four pint bottles of cream, and a bushel basket that was jumble full with bright tin cups. On the other table, four wide platters of deep-fried, homemade doughnuts sprinkled with sugar, were laid out, together with a tall stack of white paper plates and another stack of white paper napkins that were weighted down with a big smooth rock.

A dozen women stood behind one or the other of the two tables, ready to serve. They wore full-length white school-cafeteria aprons over their coats and jackets. Juanita was behind the coffee table. Her hair was tied up in a red-and-yellow, flowered scarf. She wore a black raincoat under her white apron, gray-wool slacks, and brown penny loafers. She looked up as Dub shut the motor off, and we got out.

"Come on, you men; it's ready," she called to us and the knots of hunters standing around in the parking area. The others put their guns back in their cars and pickups and moved toward the tables. Dub and I walked over, too, and got in the coffee line.

"Your wife didn't come with you?" Juanita asked her brother. He told her about Audrey having to help with a baby. Juanita turned away quickly without even speaking to me. She seemed disappointed, though I didn't know why she would be, since she'd said that she wasn't going to hunt, herself.

SEVEN

ather up a little, y'all, and I'll git us goin'," Dub called when everybody was pretty well finished with the coffee and doughnuts. He stepped over to a clear place, west of the tables and next to a little cedar tree by the seesaws. The hunters joined him over there. My dad and Stud Wampler, who'd arrived fifteen minutes or so after us, were among them.

"Folks here at 'Squahnahdale wanted me to say that they're much obliged for y'all comin' to hep 'em get shut of all these jackrabbits around here," Dub said.

I hung back by the tables and asked Juanita to pour me another cup of coffee. We hadn't talked because she hadn't at first seemed quite as friendly as she'd been at the Vernon school ground. I noticed that her hand shook a little when she handed me the hot coffee.

She took a cup, too, and then, by unspoken consent, we moved a few steps off from the other women, who were beginning to put things away.

Juanita and I backed up against the west limestone-block wall of the school building, under the eaves. The coffee was warming, going down, and the hot tin cup felt good in my hands. A light mist had started to fall, but we were mostly out of it, and the wall knocked off some of the cold wind.

"I've got to go to Cookietown, got to buy some hay," she said. Her manner seemed to warm a little with the coffee, but she didn't look directly at me. "Still want to go riding Wednesday?"

"You bet," I said. We were standing fairly close, and I caught a scent of the heavy, sweet fragrance of the Evening in Paris perfume she was wearing. It was her favorite, I knew. I'd once splurged and bought her a large, dark blue bottle of it as a birth-day present. The aroma, held close around us by the school-building wall, was for me at that moment a kind of melancholy smell, almost a funeral smell, like lilies and roses together.

"I'll haul Sugar over in a trailer, a little after noon," she said quietly. I figured that was her roan mare. "We can go from there. You're over at the Billings place, right?"

"Yeah," I said.

Our words were plain and dull, but that wasn't true of the way we were looking at each other or the way we felt standing next to each other. I was fevered by her nearness, and I couldn't make myself look away from the deep green pools of her wizard eyes.

"What?" she asked.

"A second act for us, Juanita—what're the odds on that?" I said.

"A lot's happened, Ray Lee. Let's play it out and see."

"Fair enough," I said.

And just then our attention was called back to Dub. He was announcing the ground rules for the rabbit drive.

"No twenty-twos, of course," he was saying. "Only four-tens and twenty-gauges—and twelve-gauges, too, I guess, for you boys that couldn't hit the ground with a bucket of water." Everybody laughed.

"Now, y'all know we don't never do no roundup at the end—too dangerous," Dub went on. "Even you guys that can't shoot straight might hit somebody, if we wound up in a circle. There's a little over sixty of us. So, we'll spread out for a half a mile along this south fence, here, and on the north side of the school, about a dozen yards apart, and then we'll walk abreast on a line for the three miles north to Soldier Valley School. These good ladies are gonna lay out dinner for us up there, a little after noon, and then give us rides back here.

"Now, you see, up north a ways," he said, motioning in that direction, "there's two narrow, dry-slough strips of big willers and shoemake and brush that run north and south. One slough strip is over on the left, the west, just this side of my folks' old home place, and that'll be the boundary on that side. Me and Okie'll walk over there and kinda lead up this side, the east side, of that slough." He looked around for me. "Where you at, Okie?"

"Over here," I called. I murmured to Juanita that I'd see her Wednesday, touched her lightly on the shoulder, then walked quickly over to where Dub was, by the cedar tree and the seesaws. Looking back, I saw Juanita take off her white apron and hand it to one of the community women as she got ready to leave.

"Stud, you and Hudge and some of the rest of you, there—y'all take the middle and walk up on this side, the west side, of that middle dry slough when we come to it, and, Rudy, you and Elrod and some of the rest of you, y'all split at that middle slough and go up it on its other side, on the east," Dub said. "Ever'body else kinda fill in back and forth, along the startin' fence line, here, with the highway being the boundary on the far east, of course. And the sooner we git goin', boys, the more likely we'll make it by noon up to Soldier Valley for dinner."

We all went off to collect our guns. I was empty-ing my box of thin green shotgun shells, loose, into the two side pockets of my red mackinaw when Juanita passed along the driveway in her red-and-black Jimmy pickup. I looked up and waved, but she barely nodded as she steered out to the dirt road, turned right, and sped west toward Cookietown. I turned up my coat collar and pulled down the earflaps of my cap. I wished that I'd brought gloves.

Dub and I went out to the road and walked west to the half-mile fence line. We crossed the shallow grader-ditch on the north side of the road and bent over and went through the barbed-wire fence. Near us, and all along the east–west fence line, with a temporary bulge around the school, the rest of the hunters did the same.

Everybody loaded. I opened the breech of the double-barreled 410 and inserted the two green shells I took from my right pocket, then snapped the breech shut again. Dub loaded the magazine of his pump 410.

Ready, he waved his right arm high, and the line of hunters began to move north through the native grass—gray, calf-high gramma and, in lower places, tan, knee-high buffalo grass. We could see, a quarter of a mile ahead, one on our left and the other a ways off to the right, the two low, narrow, north–south strips of woods and brush that lined the dry sloughs.

"Make a little racket," Dub hollered to the men on our right as we walked. "Pass it on!"

Along the advancing line of hunters, men shuffled their feet in the grass and stomped a little, now and then, as we moved forward.

Two big gray jackrabbits suddenly jumped up about fifty yards west of me and Dub. They zigged and zagged and leaped as they ran, spooked, their long, black-tipped ears flopping this way and that with each jerky turn and bounce.

The hunters on that part of the line cut down on them, and the noise of their shotgun blasts sounded like a half-dollar packet of giant-size Fourth of July firecrackers going off, one right after another. The two terrified rabbits didn't last a minute. Streaking at top speed when the buckshot caught them, they each dropped and tumbled through the wetting grass another couple of more lifeless yards, then lay limp and still. Hunters shouted cheers and congratulations to each other.

Most people in the county ate cottontails, but nobody I ever heard of ate jackrabbits. So we just left the dead ones where they lay—for the coyotes, someone said. Yeah, I thought to myself, if there *were* any coyotes left around there, after all the strychnining.

We kept walking north, kicking clumps of grass and making other noise as we went. More jackrabbits, one or two at a time, were scared up almost continuously, somewhere on the line. One group of hunters or another was always shooting—and shouting—and, sometimes, two or three bunches at once. You could soon smell the acrid powder smoke strongly, even with the wind.

On top of all the shotgun noise, we began to get some thunder, now and then. The clouds had lowered—and darkened. The wind was still sharp. And the misting rain was a little heavier. I wondered to myself whether we'd make it all the way to Soldier Valley before a real storm hit.

Before long, we came up to the dry slough on our left, and Dub and I and three or four others edged out ahead, along it, with our backs to the willow trees and sumac and other low bushes. Thirty yards east, my dad, Stud Wampler, and a few others were similarly edging up the west side of the other slough, more or less facing us.

Without trying to, we were all making a kind of "U" between the two narrow lines of low trees and brush, like a giant fish seine, dragging up a creek. But we were dragging the thick grass between us for jackrabbits, and, suddenly, five or six of them jumped up at the same time and raced wildly out ahead of the line, like fish before a net. Everywhere, the shotgun blasts exploded all at once, almost deafeningly.

"'Bout time *you* got one, Okie," Dub hollered. I was still without a kill. He and I raised our guns simultaneously and I cocked both hammers of mine as a couple of the rabbits veered sharply in our direction. I fired at one and felt the mild recoil against my right shoulder.

But I don't think Dub ever pulled the trigger of his 410. I heard him grunt, saw him slump, then heard another grunt from him, quick after the first one. I dropped my gun and lunged to try to grab him as he fell, face forward, into the gray grass.

"Hold it!" I yelled to the others as loud as I could, and dropped to my knees beside him. "Hold it!"

Someone nearby took up the yell. "Hold it, y'all! Stop shootin'!"

Dub was still breathing, but just barely. I rolled him over on his back. His unbuttoned jacket fell farther open, and I could see that the left side of his gray-and-black plaid shirt was badly frayed and tattered, five or six inches below his heart. The shirt-front was already soaked with blood, and the blood kept coming out and spreading.

Shooting tailed off quickly. Hunters came rushing to us, crowding around. "I'll run get my pickup," one of the younger men, nearby, said, and he and another guy took off toward Essaquahnahdale School in a hard lope.

"Dub, can you hear me?" I shouted in his face. "Hold on, now!" It seemed to me that his blue eyes were already getting set, dulling. I'd seen it in stuck hogs, the life draining out of their eyes with their blood. But Dub roused a little. His lips moved. I bent closer.

"Watch over Audrey," he said, barely audibly, then took a quick breath, and added, "Juanita."

The effort to speak made the blood flow worse.

"We'll watch over both of them," I said. "Don't talk."

And that was the last of it, the last of my old friend Dub Ready in this world. He died right there in the wet grass before they got back with the pickup.

When the truck came, we lifted his body and laid him in the back and covered him up with a wagon sheet that lay folded up there. Somebody picked up Dub's black hat and pump 410 and put them in under the tarp, too.

"Where we gonna take him?" the owner of the pickup asked as he climbed in the cab.

"To the funeral home in Vernon, I guess," I said. "I'll go tell Audrey and try to find Juanita."

It started to drizzle harder, but none of us moved from around the still-visible stain of blood on the grass.

"Shit for breakfast!" Stud said, for this moment not sounding like W.C. Fields. "How in the hell did it happen?" The question was addressed to nobody in particular.

"Must have been somebody across the way, maybe a twelve-gauge with a full choke," another man muttered, thinking aloud. Some stole glances around, but nobody owned up to having such a gun.

"Well, boys, hit's a damn shame, however it happened," my dad said. "But it sure'n hell can't be helped, now."

We stood there in shocked silence then, the rain beating down on us, until the pickup was a hundred yards or so away. At last, we all turned and trudged after it.

EIGHT

The rain had let up a little as I eased Dub's blue sheriff car into the driveway of his and Audrey's house on Church Street. The house was a well-kept white-frame, three-bedroom, just across the street east from the courthouse. The long eaves of the house hung over for nearly two feet past its walls and gave the place a faintly Chinese look.

Audrey must have been looking out the window, and she must have guessed the bad news the minute she saw me arrive without her husband. She rushed out the front door, opening a black umbrella over her head, and bounded down the porch steps while I was still getting out of the car.

She sloshed toward me, across the soppy brown Bermuda grass. "Oh no, Okie!" she cried. Her eyes were wide, her face ashen. "Oh no!"

We met at the edge of the driveway. I took her small outstretched left hand in both of mine. She was wearing a black sweater over her practical nurse's starched white uniform. A nurse's cap was pinned to her short and wavy brown hair. She had on white hose and polished white shoes. The drizzle splattered on her umbrella. She moved it a little to extend its protection to me, and, for an instant, we were silent as she read my face.

"What is it, for God's sake?" she asked.

"Shot," I said.

"And?"

"And he didn't make it, Audrey," I said. "I really hate it."

Her face crumpled. She started to cry softly, shaking. I dropped her hand, put my right arm around her tiny shoulders, and gently guided her through the light rain, back toward the house.

Inside, in the living room, we sat on a wine-colored couch with white, crocheted doilies on the arms. A healthy ivy plant sprawled across the top of the walnut coffee table. Rows of family pictures crowded the top of a baby grand piano. A framed color print of a tall-masted sailing ship in heavy seas hung on the far wall.

I told Audrey the details of Dub's death, and I said that his last words had been to ask me to watch out for her and Juanita. She covered her face with her hands and cried big sobs. I patted her on the back as soothingly as I could, though I was never good at things like that.

She sat back after a time and tried to wipe away the tears with her hands. I gave her my handkerchief.

"I just knew something bad was going to happen, Okie," she said. "Jane Gleason's baby came right away—it was her fourth—and I dropped by home for a bite of dinner before going to the hospital. I was kind of watching out the window for his car."

"Why the premonition?" I asked.

"Seems like he's been so worried lately," Audrey said. "Last night at supper, he started telling me about his business. He's never done that. Said it was just in case something should happen to him."

"You all right financially?" I asked. I did this as much to distract her as anything else. I knew that it sometimes helped people who'd suffered a death in the family to shift their focus to the problems of the living.

"My nursing job, of course," she said. "It just pays sixty-five a month, but that's something. We've got this house. He's got that quarter out by Lincoln Valley School. And there's the oil deal south of town; he was counting on that to get him square on things."

"Debts?"

A look of new distress came over her face. Her forehead wrinkled, and she looked down at her twisting hands a minute. It appeared that she was trying to decide whether or not to tell me something. Then, resolving the doubt in favor of disclosure, she raised her eyes and looked directly at me. "Okie, Dub was running around—and gambling a lot," she said.

"Whereabouts?"

"Up at Lawton, the Idle Hour Club," she said.

"That old place still going?" I said.

"I knew he was under some kind of pressure," Audrey went on, "but he didn't tell me until last night what a hole he was in. Some bad people were threatening him."

I couldn't think of anything to say. We sat without speaking for a while.

Finally, she said, "I've got some coffee on the stove, if you want some."

I thanked her and said I did. She gave me back my handkerchief, crossed to the dining room, and pushed through a swinging door into the kitchen. I got up and walked over to the piano and looked idly through the photographs. I picked up a glamorous

eight-by-ten graduation picture of Juanita and realized again that I was going to have to find her and
tell her, too, about Dub's death. I didn't look forward
to it.

Audrey returned and put the coffee cups on the
table in front of the couch. We sat back down.

"Had a will, I guess?" I said. My law training
coming out.

"Silliest thing," she said. "Juanita was after Dub
until we had one made and signed it a couple of
weeks ago. We never had kids. . . ."

She started to cry again and used one of the
white-linen napkins she'd brought in with the coffee
to blot her eyes.

In a little while, she continued. "Both our parents
are gone, mine died in the 1918 flu epidemic, you
know, when I was little. Not much use for a will—
but, anyway, it's a joint one. Says that if Dub dies
first, everything goes to me, and if I die first, everything goes to him."

Audrey cried hard again for a time. Once more,
still feeling awkward, I tried to help by gently pat-
ting her on the shoulder.

The doorbell rang. We both got up. Audrey went
to the front door and admitted a neighbor woman, a
Mrs. Walters, the wife of one of the men at the rabbit
drive. She was a heavyset woman with a schoolteacher's rimless glasses. She carried a red-glass
bowl with an embroidered white tea cloth draped
over it. Her blue overcoat was pulled up over her
head for protection from the drizzle. She took it
down and straightened it.

"So awfully sorry, Audrey, to hear the terrible
news," the woman said. The two of them embraced,
the visitor holding the bowl out to the side in her
right hand. When they stepped back from each
other, the woman handed the bowl to Audrey. "I

brought you some pea salad," she said. There was something about a death that seemed instantly to set Vernon women to preparing covered dishes.

Audrey took the bowl and thanked Mrs. Walters. She turned and introduced me, then, and invited the woman to come in and sit a while, and have coffee.

I followed Audrey back to the kitchen, where she put the pea salad in the Frigidaire and poured a cup to take back to Mrs. Walters.

"If you'll tell me where Juanita lives, I guess I ought to go and tell her," I said.

"Oh, that Juanita!" Audrey said. She was obviously put out. "She's been such a trial, encouraging Dub in his running around and gambling, going with him a lot to Lawton—and always needing money herself. Lately, though, she's been mad at him for not letting her in on the oil deal."

Then Audrey seemed to think better of what she'd said. Her tone softened. "Well, poor thing," she said, "I shouldn't say anything bad about her. Lord knows she's had more than her share of life's troubles."

Our eyes met. "I'm sorry," she said. "I didn't mean you."

She gave me directions to Juanita's house, then, and walked me back to the front door, pausing along the way to hand the full coffee cup to Mrs. Walters. I hugged Audrey close. She held me for what seemed like a full minute.

"We never quit thinking of you as our best old friend," she said. I bent over and kissed her on the forehead. "Go ahead and take Dub's car, Okie," she said. "And do you think you could come back and carry me down to the funeral home later? I don't want to go by myself."

I said I'd be glad to.

NINE

Juanita lived on the north edge of Vernon, down Main Street and across the highway, two blocks north of the Truckers Cafe. I had no trouble picking out the corner house.

Her red-and-black Jimmy was sitting in the gravel driveway. Jumbled in the bed of the pickup truck were three bales of gray-green alfalfa, darker on top where the hay was wet.

I parked on the Main Street side of the nice little rock house. In back, I could see a small, corrugated-tin barn and an adjoining welded-pipe horse lot where her strawberry-roan mare stood watching me as I got out of the car. A blue, metal, two-horse trailer was parked beside the barn.

I walked to the front door, which was flanked by two large juniper sentinels. Juanita opened the door as soon as I knocked.

"Juanita . . ." I said through the screen door, not knowing quite how to begin.

"I know, Ray Lee," she interrupted, her green eyes examining me intently. "Come on in."

She held open the screen door and the main door,

and I went in. All the shades were drawn. The living room was dark, except for a light that came from the entrance to the kitchen. I could see, though, that her normally pale face was flushed, as if rouged. Her eyes were red, her long black hair wet. She wore a floor-length, black, high-necked Chinese silk robe, cinched at the waist, and was shoeless.

Wordlessly, she took my damp mackinaw and hung it up on a hook behind the front door. She motioned me toward an overstuffed chair, then came over and sat down, herself, on the adjacent divan, at the end nearest me. Both the divan and chair were covered in the same, too-cheerful print material that featured giant white daisies splashed on a bright yellow background. And at the right angle where the divan and chair came together, there was a low light-oak end table with a painted-plaster reading lamp in the shape of a rearing horse.

I saw that Juanita was drinking. There was a quart bottle of Ancient Age bourbon, two-thirds gone, on the light-oak coffee table in front of us and, next to the bottle, a heavy water glass, half-full of what looked like straight whiskey.

She picked up this drink and then, abruptly and without drinking from it, set it right back down again. She jumped up nervously, crossed over to an open oak breakfront, and took out a matching glass.

"You probably need a shot, too," she said, coming back. She stooped, picked up the bottle of Ancient Age, and filled the glass about a third of the way up with the brown bourbon. She held it out to me. I took it. She wore a large diamond ring on her right hand, a small jade one on her left.

Standing right in front of me, she reached down again and picked up the green package of Lucky Strikes from the coffee table, shook out one, and stuck it between her lips. I noticed that her lipstick had worn off. She dropped the cigarette package, then took up a silver lighter and handed it to me, bending down so I could light her cigarette.

As I did so, our eyes met provocatively for an instant. Despite the sad circumstances, it was a charged moment like when Clark Gable and Claudette Colbert first looked at each other in that suddenly knowing way in *It Happened One Night*.

Juanita straightened up, took a long drag on her Lucky Strike, and then, as before, seated herself on the front edge of the couch, at the end nearest me. I put the lighter back on the coffee table, lifted my glass, and took a stiff swig. The bourbon was harsh going down. I coughed and then shivered.

Juanita picked up her own glass. Her hand trembled as she took a long drink. She saw that I noticed the shaking. Her black-leather purse was on the couch to the left of her. She set down her glass, opened the purse flap, and fished out a dark medicine bottle, about half-pint size. I knew it was a paregoric bottle; you could find them in people's trash when I was a kid and sell them for a penny each.

She unscrewed the cap, put the bottle to her lips, and took a big gulp. Then, replacing the lid, she stuffed the bottle back in her purse. Afterward, she deliberately picked up her whiskey glass and took two strong swallows of it without flinching.

"What's in the bottle?" I asked.

"Bourbon, of course," she said with a sly smile, taking a drag from her cigarette.

"The other bottle."

"Paregoric," she said. "Doc Watson gives it to me for my nerves."

"Good idea to chase it with Ancient Age?" I asked.

"Making some kind of health survey, are you, Ray Lee?" she countered.

I changed the subject. "You've had a lot of deaths, Juanita," I said, meaning to be consoling, "and I'm truly sorry."

"You're right, Ray Lee," she said. Her eyes were sad. She looked directly at me as she spoke. She seemed calmer than she'd been at first, almost languid.

Her gaze shifted to her glass, and she downed another swallow of whiskey. I took my second swig and shivered again, even though I was beginning to feel warm.

"Your folks, first, and now Dub," I said.

"And the baby," she added, very softly. She lowered her eyes and stared blankly into her glass.

I wasn't sure I'd heard right. I flushed. I was conscious of my heartbeat. "What do you mean, the baby?" I asked.

"I had an abortion," she said in a quiet voice. She was detached, as if she were relating a dream or a thing that had happened to someone else. "Ray Lee, I never went to a home in St. Louis. I moved in with my aunt Maude, my dad's black-sheep sister there— she died last year—and she arranged for a witch of an old woman to come to her house and do it. It was awful."

I sucked in my breath, stunned. A wave of intense and confused feelings crashed over me—an odd stir of relief that at least I didn't have a child out in the world somewhere, on its own, a bleak sadness at an unexpected loss, and, over it all, a sharp sense of renewed guilt.

When I spoke, my voice sounded hoarse. "I'm sorry to have caused you to have to go through all that," I said. I had never meant anything more sincerely. And I felt like I ought to try, somehow, to make things better for her.

She set her glass down and slowly snuffed her

cigarette out in a ceramic-saddle ashtray on the coffee table. Then she patted the couch beside her with her left hand and stretched out her right toward me, beckoning.

"Come here," she said. "It certainly was more my own fault than anybody's."

She didn't have to ask twice. I was beside her on the couch at once. She turned to me and took me in her arms. It was an embrace that seemed to begin for both of us as an act of comfort. But, in an instant, it became another thing altogether—ardent, fervid. We kissed hotly.

The robe came undone easily, and she was naked underneath it. I didn't even undress. We never left the couch. We made love right there in her dark living room like heedless high-school kids, out of control.

TEN

Stigler-Martin Funeral Home was built like a rambling, ranch-style frame house. It covered most of two lots at the corner of Icehouse Street and Church Street, a block east of the bank.

A little bell hanging inside on the front door tinkled sharply as Audrey and I entered.

Greg Martin came at once to the reception room. Tall and lean, he wore a black, three-piece suit. His dark hair was parted in the middle and slicked down with Vitalis, as it had always been when we were at Vernon High School together. Back then, we'd called him Deacon because, even as an apprentice undertaker, he had a preacher's formal and solicitous manner. Some kids in school had thought he was a little weird to be working at the funeral home, but I'd always found him a pretty nice guy.

Greg and I shook hands and said hello. Then he took Audrey's hand in both his and held it. "I am truly sorry, Audrey," he said. His manner was solemn and sympathetic, the formality of it, I figured, a kind of learned defense against letting people's grief get too close to him.

"She'd like to see him, Greg," I said.

He dropped Audrey's hand and stepped back. "We don't yet have the body ready for viewing," he said apologetically. "Perhaps y'all would like to come back first thing in the morning."

"No, Greg," Audrey said quietly, but forcefully. "I want to see him now."

"All right, then, Audrey," Martin agreed, becoming less formal. "But y'all wait here. It'll take me a little while."

He went down a long hall and through a door at the back. Audrey and I sank into heavily padded chairs.

There were two viewing rooms off the long hall that led from the reception area. The one on the left was in use, we could tell. A little boy near Lincoln Valley, we learned later from Greg Martin, had died the day before from a mule's kick to the head. Some of his folks were sitting up with the body for the night. The sickeningly heavy fragrance of lilies and other funeral flowers coming from that room put me back at the funeral service for my mother and made me feel uncomfortable.

Audrey and I sat silently for several minutes. Finally, Greg returned. We followed him to the other viewing chamber, on the right side of the hall.

He'd brought Dub Ready's body into the room from a rear door that led to the embalming lab. Dub was laid out on a wheeled table with a fringed white skirt around it. A quilted, white-satin comforter, draped over a white sheet, covered the body. Only the face was exposed, the eyes closed. Dub's red hair was still in some disarray. His face looked gaunt, the skin waxy and gray.

Audrey didn't break down. She stood very close to the body, looking down at Dub's face and crying softly. I was a half step behind her, Greg Martin at the door. Audrey touched Dub's cheek for an instant, then drew her hand back rather quickly in an apparent reaction to the unnaturally cold skin.

"Poor baby, poor baby," she said quietly.

We stayed only five or ten minutes. Greg Martin walked us back toward the front. But before we reached the reception area, he pulled me aside for a moment, as Audrey continued on.

"Okie, Doc Watson's death certificate's wrong," he said in a low voice. "He just rushed over here for a minute after I called him, drinking I think, and asked a couple of questions of the boy who brought the body in. Then he wrote down that the cause of death was a shotgun shot—singular—to the chest. But, Okie, Dub wasn't shot in the chest. He was shot in the back."

"In the back?" I asked, incredulous.

"Twice."

"Twice?"

"Twice—and by a rifle."

"Are you sure?" I asked.

"I want you to come take a look," Greg said.

I told him I'd be back in a moment. I took Audrey to Dub's car—I was still driving it—and asked her to wait a few minutes for me. I told her that Greg wanted to talk with me about arrangements.

Greg waited for me in the viewing room, then led me back into the adjoining lab, where he'd already rolled Dub's body. The unclothed body on the wheeled table was covered only with a brown, rubberized sheet, the cloth sheet and quilted comforter having been removed and put away.

I wasn't happy about having to do it, but I steeled myself and looked at the body as Greg pulled back the covering from Dub's chest. The skin below the ribs on his left side was torn and shredded around a ragged wound that was as wide around as a coffee mug. The blood in and circling the wound had dried dark, like bottomland mud.

"That's an exit wound," Greg said. He put on some rubber gloves. "Now, help me turn him on his side and look at this."

I assisted with what was for me a really distasteful job, being careful to touch only the brown sheet. Greg steadied Dub Ready's stiff white body with one gloved hand and pointed with the other. The two holes in Dub's back were small, the puckered skin around them dark purple.

"Here, in about the middle of the back on the left side is one bullet hole," Greg said. "And, there, slightly lower in the back on the same side, is another."

"They're entry wounds, and from a rifle," I said.

"You're right about that. Looks like maybe twenty-two-caliber bullets."

Reality had totally changed, like when you look at one of those trick black-and-white pictures one way, and it's just clouds, and then you look at it another way, and suddenly it's a drawing of Jesus or something.

"The first shot must have been the one that hit him higher, here, in his back, I imagine," I said, "the second, a little lower, after he started to fall."

"So, what do you think, Okie?"

"Great heavenly shit!" I said. "What do I think? I think somebody murdered him." The realization hit me hard.

"What should we do?" Greg asked, as we laid the body back down.

"The first thing is to get Doc Watson back over here to make out a correct report," I said. "I've gotta take Audrey on home. But you make sure Doc Watson's sober—or get him sober."

ELEVEN

Late Sunday afternoon, the First Methodist Church was full. It was pretty quick to have a funeral, but there'd been no relatives from out of town to wait for, and Stigler-Martin already had two funerals booked for Monday.

My dad, Stud Wampler, and I sat in the middle section of the church, about halfway back. Down front, Dub Ready's gray metallic casket rested on a wheeled stand in front of the pulpit. Audrey, Juanita, and other relatives and closest friends sat in the first two rows.

There were great banks of funeral sprays and flower baskets on each side of the coffin. The sun's rays through the two giant stained-glass windows cast a strange red-tinted kind of light around the church sanctuary.

The preacher's wife sang a querulous-soprano rendition of "Lead, Kindly Jesus." The portly Reverend Tom Mildren then stepped to the lectern and began to speak in appropriately solemn tones.

"Brothers and sisters," he said, "in John 14, we have the words of Our Lord to comfort us in this time of trouble." Reverend Mildren didn't need to consult the open Bible in front of him as he recited the familiar words from memory, as most of us who'd grown up on scripture could, too. "Jesus said: 'In my Father's house are many mansions; if it were not so, I would have told you. I go to prepare a place for you—that where I am, there ye may be also.'"

As Reverend Mildren then preached on that theme for a time, though not as long as a Baptist preacher would have, my mind wandered to the most basic questions I'd been thinking about ever since I'd looked at Dub Ready's body at the funeral home. How? Who? Why? I still couldn't find any answers and finally came on back to the service as the minister began to wind up on a personal note.

"J.W. Ready was a good man," he said. "Many of you may not know that he had been growing closer to his church in recent months. And very few of you are aware of all the private charity he did, not wanting it known. Of the elderly lady whose gallbladder operation he paid for out of his own pocket. Of his paying for the gasoline himself to carry a little boy to Crippled Childrens Hospital in Oklahoma City. He was a good man, and he will be missed, here in Vernon."

The organ began to play. Quietly, Greg Martin and another male attendant from Stigler-Martin came down front and propped open the casket lid. The two then each took an aisle, and, with family members remaining seated, ushered others of the audience forward, row by row, to view the body and, then, file out of the church.

I'd always hated the part of a funeral where you have to look at the dead person, and I made short work of it, walking by the coffin with hardly a glance. Afterward, Stud, my dad, and I joined the others outside, at the front of the church. We waited,

hats in our hands, until the casket, followed by
Audrey, Juanita, and other family members—two
second cousins and their wives, mainly—finally
emerged.

Juanita seemed to be even more broken up than
Audrey. They both wore black veils over their faces.
Still, their great distress was obvious. I wanted to go
to Juanita, but decided against it.

The casket was carried down the steps by the
pallbearers and loaded into the waiting black hearse.
Family members got into the lined-up big cars the
funeral home had provided. The crowd began to dis-
perse to their own cars to join the cortege.

I was turning to leave when Marsh Traynor came
up from behind and took my arm.

"You goin' out the cemetery, come ride with me,"
he said as he covered his bald head with a narrow-
brim Stetson. Traynor's voice was much lower than
usual, his round, red face more serious. "Got somethin' I need to talk with you about."

Curious, I told my dad and Stud Wampler to go
on without me and walked around the corner with
Traynor to a big, black, four-door Buick Roadmaster
with white sidewall tires. It looked like a gangster
car from a Jimmy Cagney movie.

There were just the two of us. I got in on the passenger side. He eased his stout body in under the
steering wheel, inserted and turned the key, and
pressed his foot on the starter pedal. The big engine
growled hoarsely into action. After two or three minutes, Traynor eased off the clutch, turned the corner
onto Church Street, and directed the weighty auto-
mobile into the moving line behind the family cars,
about a half-dozen places back from the hearse. We
would go north on Church Street, down to the highway, then head west for the mile-and-a-half drive to
the Vernon Cemetery.

Steering with one hand, Traynor took a ready-roll Chesterfield from a package on the dash, lit it with a kitchen match that he ignited with his thumb, then began.

"Okie, I'll get right to the point," he said, his usual roar back, even in the close confines of the car. "The County Commission wants you to take over as sheriff. You the best man for the job, and we'd like to appoint you, first thing tomorrow morning, to fill out Dub Ready's term."

The offer caught me completely by surprise. I'd not had the least shaving of an idea that Traynor might want to talk with me about such a thing. I could hear my dad saying, "Any sumbitch ever totes a gun never wants to do nothin' else!"

"You think I look like a gun toter?" I said.

"Your deputies can carry the guns," Traynor said. "And you can name whoever you want as chief deputy. We already run off that chickenshit Merkle that Dub had, part of a deal tryin' to shake me down. He lit out for Bakersfield."

"Shouldn't a guy be able to grow a decent set of whiskers before you make him a sheriff?" I said. I wondered what Traynor meant about a shakedown.

"You pert near the same age as Dub—and Cash County likes givin' a young man a chance. You got law trainin', and it's a way to make a livin'. Pays a hundred dollars a month, and we'll buy that car off of Audrey for you."

"Fellow can't get fat on a wage like that," I said.

"We'll agree to let you keep on tradin' some, on the side."

"Somebody murdered Dub Ready, Mr. Traynor," I said. "And they oughta be caught and sent to the electric chair."

"Mighty right about that."

"And I know about as much about crime detection as I know about whaling," I said.

"Much as anybody, and you learn faster'n most."

"Who knows where the trail of Dub's killer might lead?" I said. "He had enemies."

"Near 'bout as many as his old man," Traynor said. "And you gotta put me in that dern category, too, for both of them."

"Wasn't talking about you," I said.

"Take this here job, Okie, and you can follow the trail wherever she leads," Traynor said. "Don't make no difference. Main thing, study about it, talk it over with Hudge, if you want to, and meet me and the other two commissioners down at the courthouse by eight tomorrow morning, if you decide to do it—and I sure as hell hope you will."

I thought about something else then. "Any way you could clean up the mud in old man Nahnah-pwa's pond?" I asked.

"Who told you about my drilling out there?" Traynor said, as if surprised by my bringing up the subject. "Dub say somethin' to you?"

"He did mention it," I said, stopping there. I thought there was no use saying anything about Dub wanting me to get the Indian to sign oil leases. "But it was old man Nahnahpwa, himself, that ask me to speak to you about cleaning up his pond."

"I'll take care of that, Okie," Traynor said quickly. "Thought my boys already had."

After the short and cold graveside service at the windswept cemetery, I hugged Audrey and Juanita in turn and expressed my condolences again. I crawled into my dad's old pickup with him and Stud Wampler, and we headed back to town.

I told them what Traynor had wanted.

"Any sumbitch ever totes a gun never wants to do nothin' else!" my dad said.

"It'd be some security," I said.

"Shit, if it's security you after, why don't you just go to the pen and be done with it?" he said.

"Traynor'll let me name my own chief deputy, and he said I could keep on tradin' on the side."

"Hudge, old sport," Stud said in his best W.C. Fields nasal drawl, "it would appear to a casual observer that our boy, Okie, here, has stumbled upon what might rightly be designated a bird nest on the ground."

My dad was not convinced. "On one thing or 'nother, probably wind up havin' to arrest some a you own kinfolks or close friends," he said.

"I wouldn't be a damned bit surprised," I said.

TWELVE

I took two quick actions Monday morning, right after I was sworn in as sheriff and signed the payroll. One was to turn Poss Tatums out of jail. The other was to hire Stud Wampler as my chief deputy for $90 a month, the full amount allowed for the job by the County Commission.

I told Marsh Traynor and the other Cash County commissioners in advance about both things I wanted to do. They raised no objections. We shook hands all around, and the three of them and Justice of the Peace Marney, who'd sworn me in, left me alone in the office with Crystal Boucher.

This tall and skinny woman, the kind Mama would have called gawky, was my whole office staff—secretary, office manager, receptionist, and phone answerer. And she did all that, I found out from looking at the books, for $52 a month.

But Crystal was a cheerful person by nature, God alone knew why, given her circumstances. I introduced myself to her, and we got acquainted quickly.

It was clear that she hadn't been blowing her wages on clothes. Her plain cotton dress had obviously made a few too many trips to the help-yourself laundry or the home washtub and rub-board. Her low-cut brown shoes were run over at the heels. She looked underfed, too, and probably was, I figured, after I heard more of her story.

Crystal was little more than five years older than me, but her hair was already graying, and it was no wonder. Her husband, Ike Boucher, had been killed the year before when a steam engine he was driving, pulling a threshing machine, had broken through a plank bridge, crashed off sideways, and landed upside down on top of him. That left Crystal to raise their fifth-grader daughter by herself.

"Your folks living with you, too?" I asked. That's what I'd heard. There was just four rooms to the old hull of a farmhouse that she rented northeast of town, near Lincoln Valley School. She drove into work in a rusted model-A Ford Ike had left her.

"Mama's got arthritis so bad in her hands that she cain't do people's sewin' no more," Crystal said. "And Daddy stays so down in his back all the time that he cain't work on the county road grader. They both still not old enough for the old-age pension. Daddy goes into town with a wagon and team and hauls back garbage that the cafés save for him and feeds out a few hogs with it. Sometimes, there's even things like oranges and, maybe, bread that we can eat, our ownselves. We make do, and the Lord has been good to let me still have my folks this long."

"I don't see how you can make it on the little dab the sheriff's office pays," I said.

"Could be worse," she said. She shrugged and bent to take a large ring of keys and a thin, bound record book from her middle desk drawer.

"How?"

"If it was any more, we wouldn't be eligible to draw them free commodities," she said. "Now, we are. Look on the bright side, that's what Ike always said."

"Ike must have carried a big lantern," I said.

Crystal showed me the record book on the prisoners we had in custody—two men from Randlett, who were charged with stealing a wagonload of wheat out of a farmer's granary, and the Wardell Negro, Poss Tatums. She gave me the jail keys.

The sheriff's office was on the third floor of the courthouse. The jail was three iron-bar cages, farther up a half flight of concrete steps, in a kind of attic, under the slanted tin roof. A heavy metal door guarded the stairs to the jail. I lifted the iron rod that barred it, swung open the door, and headed up. The stairwell was chilly. The jail had to be an icebox in winter, I figured, and hotter than a two-dollar cookstove in summer.

In one of two back cells, the alleged grain thieves, middle-aged, stubble-faced, their hair like rats' nests, sat on their bunks and stared sullenly at me without speaking. Tatums was in the nearer, front cell, dozing on a busted cotton pad on a pull-down iron bed frame. He sat up slowly and rubbed his eyes, watching me. The first two keys I tried on his cell door didn't work.

"Hit's the big brassy one, boss," Tatums said.

He was right. I opened the cell door and stepped just inside.

"You the man, now." He said this matter-of-factly or, perhaps, with a hint of mockery in his voice. I couldn't tell which. Then he dropped his gaze to his big hands, which were folded in the lap of his worn Blue Bell overalls. Back in the servile role.

I looked down at the silvery sheriff's badge on my left shirt pocket, then back at him. He was as black as Marfak axle grease, his hair nappy and matted. What should have been the whites of his eyes were yellowish, and there was a long, raised scar along his right jawline. He couldn't have been more than forty, I thought, but his worn-out face and tired slump made him seem much older.

"What are you in here for?" I asked.

"Boss, you know I's in here for nothin' atall," he said. "I hope you gon' turn pore old Poss aloose and 'low me to git back to my wife and chirrens." This last he said in an affected, pitiful voice.

"Get back to your whores and gamblin', more likely," I said. I wasn't totally comfortable with such a stern tone, but I continued on with it, anyway. "Now, they arrested you for deviant sex with that white man, ain't that right?"

"Nawsir, all due respect," Tatums said. He turned and looked down toward the cell where the other two inmates sat. Then he lowered his voice and went on. "Sheriff and that deputy Merkle set it all up. Next time that white man comes wantin' a woman, they says to me, call 'em and stall the man and tell 'im you goin' wid 'im to git a hotel room. Then, they says, go up to the room myself and take off my over-halls quick. That's when them two busts in with that big Kodak got a flash on it."

"You sayin' it was a frame-up to blackmail the white man?" I asked.

He looked straight at me, almost defiant. "If I be queer, boss, I kiss your ass," he said.

"Not the best expression to use in your denial," I said.

"Suh?"

"Never mind," I said. "What'd *you* get out of it—playing along with Mr. Ready and Merkle?"

"Say they won't send old Poss to the pen for this and that," he said. The pitiful tone had returned.

"Who's the white man you framed?"

"Man gon' kill me, I tell you that," Tatums said.

"Maybe done already killed Sheriff Ready, fer as I know."

"You done this before for Mr. Ready?" I asked.

"Oncet," he said. "And this here second time—hit was shore oncet too many."

"Get your coat and cap, and follow me," I said.

I took Tatums downstairs. Crystal allowed him to call somebody in Wardell who he said was a family member to come and get him. She gave him back his billfold. He put on his gray-wool cap and his well-worn brown suit coat. She motioned him to a chair to wait.

I put on my Stetson and mackinaw to leave. Tatums stood up again, yanking his cap off, when he saw that I was getting ready to go.

"Ol' Poss is sure much obliged to you, boss, Mr. Sheriff," he said. "You mind shaking hands with a colored?"

We shook hands. "Go and sin no more," I said.

I left to find Stud.

THIRTEEN

Stud Wampler was not on the corner in front of Herschel Brothers Drugstore with the other cow traders when I drove by. Neither was my dad. Lots of mornings, my dad stopped by Grandma Dunn's little two-room house on Ohio Street to drop her off some eggs or something and to check up on her. Two or three times a week, Stud met him there, and they had a cup of Grandma's stout coffee before setting out on another day of trading.

I headed to Grandma's. Both my dad's old green Ford truck and Stud's yellow Dodge were out front, on the street. I parked the sheriff's blue Ford V-Eight sedan behind them, went around to the side of Grandma's house, opened the back door without knocking, and stepped up into the cramped little beige-wallpapered kitchen. Dad and Stud had only just seated themselves at the four-place, white-enamel table. It was covered with a red-and-white-checked oilcloth and nearly filled all the kitchen floor space.

"How's everybody this morning?" I said cheerfully, and took off my Stetson and laid it on top of the wooden icebox with the other two.

"Just in time, Okie, for some coffee—and some hoecakes, too, if you want 'em," Grandma said. My dad's mother was a hard-shell Baptist, a thin and stern old widow woman with sparse white hair done up in a bun. She turned to get another cup from the movable cabinet. I declined the hoecakes.

Grandma Dunn was a woman whose sad gray eyes were perpetually fixed on heaven. She was just waiting, as she put it, often, for the Lord to "call her on home" to her reward. She sang or whistled hymns nearly all the time, never secular songs. The words of her favorite church song went: "This world is not my home; I'm only passing through." And that was her philosophy.

I said hello and sat down at the table with Stud and my dad. The friendship between those two went way back and was as strong as Old Nellie's breath, as my dad would have said. I remembered being with them one time when they were both on a crying drunk, and Stud, slumping over my dad and hugging him, had slurred out, "I just love this little sumbitch. If he tells you a rooster can pull a house, you better go git the harness."

Grandma Dunn hummed snatches of her favorite hymn as she poured my coffee from the blue-porcelain pot she took from the low, red-and-yellow flame of one of her coal-oil stove's smelly front burners.

She brought over the steaming chipped brown mug, then picked up the small basket of brown eggs my dad had just brought in with him. She turned, bent down, and opened the icebox door with her free hand, took the eggs, one by one, and carefully rowed them up inside the icebox on the top shelf.

"Needin' ice; gonna have to put the ten-pound card up in the window, so the iceman'll stop," she said, more or less to herself, and handed my dad's basket back to him. That done, she wasted no time in launching right into her usual reproach about trading cattle.

"I reckon you still tradin' cows, son," she said to my dad with a kind of sorrowful resignation. "And, now, seems like you gittin' you own boy in it, to boot. You know hit's speckalation, jes pure-dee ol' gamblin'."

My dad grinned, a little lopsidedly. His nose had been busted more than once and was somewhat off center in his Scots-Irish red face. He'd heard this same lecture a hundred times. "Cow tradin' ain't gambling the way I do it, Ma," he said.

He was right. The third grade was as far as my dad ever got in school. But there weren't a whole lot of people who could—accurately and in their heads, as he could when he was sober—make the complicated estimates and calculations and judgments required to buy a load of cattle worth the money and then resell them at a profit.

The gang of full-time cow traders in Vernon—there were eight of us, after I'd joined up—could do that. But, with the possible exception of Stud Wampler, none quite as skillfully as my dad. And most of us, unlike my dad, had to use a pencil and scratch paper to do the necessary figuring.

Every morning, early, you listened to the market reports on the radio. How much a hundredweight were the various grades of cattle going for at the Oklahoma City market—stocker calves, say, or fat steers, or the older cows they called "canners and cutters"? You bought cattle from farmers—in the field or cow lot or at one of the several nearby weekly auction sales. Then you hauled them, or had them hauled, the 120 miles northeast to the Oklahoma City Stockyards, and hoped you could get rid of them there for enough to make some money.

For my dad, doing all that, cow trading, was not the same as gambling, at least not most of the time. With him, it was more like a science.

"No, ma'am, Miz Dunn, for Hudge it's buyin' goats that can prove to be a game of chance," Stud said. He wasn't wearing the tall hat of Mr. McCawber in *David Copperfield*, but his voice sounded uncannily like that of W.C. Fields, who played McCawber in that picture show. Stud was built big, like Fields, too, though he didn't have Fields's bulbous red nose. He didn't look up from his coffee when he said this.

Grandma didn't get Stud's reference to goats. My dad and I did. He grinned, and I laughed right out loud.

If my dad got to drinking more than he could handle, which he didn't do too often, he might show up at a sale barn and try to buy everything that came through the ring, worth the money or not. Stud's allusion was to a time, several years earlier, when my dad had bought a semitrailer truckload of long-haired goats—and he hated goats! "Lost my ass and all the fixtures on them goats," my dad had admitted to me later, embarrassed.

"Glad you not still studyin' to make a lawyer, Okie," Grandma Dunn said to me, then. "Lord knows, even cow tradin' beats that. But I heared, now, you fixin' to be the sheriff."

"Just got through taking the oath, Grandma," I said. "On a Bible, you'll be glad to know."

"Cain't hurt," she said.

My dad lit up a Camel, and the first lungful of smoke started him on a coughing fit, his face turning redder even than usual as he fought to get his breath. We waited.

"Them coffin nails gonna kill you, son," Grandma

Dunn said when he'd quieted. Dad took a sip of his coffee.

To no one in particular, Stud started a recitation in his W.C. Fields voice: "It wasn't the cough that carried him off; it was the coffin they carried him off'n."

"Well, we ain't makin' a dime settin' here," my dad said abruptly, and pushed back from the little table. Stud and I got up, too, and we all picked up our hats and put them on. "Needin' anything else, Ma?" Dad asked as he turned to leave.

"Naw, son, but I sure do thank you fer them eggs," she said. "Hope that old farewell-office biddy, old lady Pearson, don't try and count 'em agin me. Always snoopin' around, tryin' to catch me makin' a little extry from ironin' for people, so she kin dock my old-age pension. Y'all come again, now."

She didn't walk us to the door, but busily set about picking up the coffee cups. There were no hugs, either. We weren't the kind that showed affection much.

Stud and my dad and I walked out to my dad's old truck. I told them what I'd come for, that I wanted to hire Stud as my chief deputy. I said that the salary was only $90, but that we could both keep on trading.

"Masked man, stud," Stud said solemnly, extending his hand to me for a shake on the deal, "you have just hired yourself a loyal Tonto."

"Totin' a gun!" my dad said dismissively.

"He doesn't have to carry a gun," I said. "I'm not."

"I am," Stud said. "No man with a jaw made by Waterford should rely only on his fists. I'm plannin' on packin' the largest piece of hardware I can find in Cash County."

My dad and a couple of other Vernon guys had

once trained Stud, when he was young, to be heavy-weight boxing's next "great white hope." And Stud was pretty good, too, I'd heard. Big and rawboned, rough, he'd learned rapidly to be a pretty good prizefighter. The only trouble was that he'd turned out to have a glass jaw. He was an easy knockout, if he got hit just right. And, too many times, apparently, that's just what had happened.

"Yessir, studs, I'm gonna carry a damn big hog-leg," Stud said. "And the jawbone of an ass, too, if she's legal."

I asked him to leave his truck and ride out with me to Essaquahnahdale to have a new look, together, at the place where Dub Ready had been killed. I was determined to get to the bottom of that murder as soon as possible.

FOURTEEN

We left the sheriff car in the gravel parking lot at Essaquahnahdale School and had no trouble picking out and following from there the twin tire tracks that had been left in the wet pasture by the pickup that had hauled off Dub's body. The imprints were still quite apparent.

And despite the rain that had started on that Saturday, it was still pretty easy for us to find the spot at the end of the pickup tracks where Dub had gone down. The grass was still flattened there and where we'd all stood around the body. Knowing what to look for, Stud and I even made out some of the remaining stain of Dub's blood on the ground in the center of the site.

I positioned the two of us pretty much where Dub and I had been when he was shot. Stud and I faced east. Our backs were toward the willows and sumac and other brush of the dry slough behind us—though, as we were to find, with the long and soaking rain that'd come, the slough wasn't dry anymore.

"Dub was shot in the back—twice," I said, turning to look behind us at the slough. "Somebody had to be hiding in that brush back there."

Stud wondered whether we ought to try to look on the ground where Dub was shot to see if we could find the .22 bullet that had exited the body.

"Naw," I said, "that would be like trying to find a chigger on a possum. Let's go see if we can tell where the killer stood and try to find some foot-prints."

It was quick work. With no trouble, we found the killer's hiding place, the only clear space, it turned out, that could have been used along the east bank of the slough. It was a concealed sitting place on a cou-ple of crossed logs, back in the brush, maybe thirty yards from where Dub had been hit. Stud and I saw that the killer would have been well shielded from the view of all of us hunters by a large hackberry bush and some sumac in front. The rifle would have been sighted over the bush, and could have been steadied just right, we figured, on a limb of a willow tree growing up through the bush.

I told Stud to go out and stand in the pasture, with his back to me, on the spot where Dub had been when he was shot, while I sighted on him from the killer's point of view. When he returned, I said, "The shots wouldn't have been totally easy, but, for an experienced shooter, they wouldn't have been totally difficult, either. The killer waited until we'd all walked on past a ways and had to be using a semiautomatic rifle, the shots came so close together."

We found no tracks in the hiding place. Under and around the killer's seat was a thick spread of Bermuda grass, not soft dirt that might have retained impressions. Stud and I looked around carefully, but we found no .22 shell casings, either. The killer had obviously been careful enough to pick them up. Neither were there any cigarette butts, if the killer was a smoker and had lit up while waiting for us.

What had the killer done after firing? "Must have hunkered down here like a newborn calf 'til we'd all left," Stud said. "Figured rightly that we'd think the shots came from one of the hunters."

We did find what might have been foot tracks that seemed to lead from the hiding place back down to the slough's new waterline, into what had been a dry bed a few days earlier. But the rain had made the tracks unreadable.

"Might be the killer's," Stud said, "or just some kid's, playin' here, sometime or 'nother, or huntin' rabbits."

Across the slough and through the willows on the other side, to the west, we could see the weathered, shingle-roofed barn of what had been the old Hoyt Ready place. Next to the barn, a rock foundation was all that remained of the burned house.

"How'd the Readys kill themselves?" I asked Stud as we turned and started walking back toward Essaquahnahdale School.

"Shot," he said.

"Shot?" This was a surprise to me. I guess I'd imagined that the cause of their deaths was something else—poison, maybe. "They shot themselves after they set the fire?"

"That's what was said," Stud replied.

"I mean, did Hoyt shoot Inez and then himself, or what?" I asked.

"Lone Ranger stud," Stud said, back in his W.C. Fields voice, "the possessor of that information, if such exists in *this* world, has never vouchsafed it to us mortals."

"Must have been an investigation and a coroner's report," I said. "Had to be."

"The eminent Dr. Watson signed the official report," Stud said. "He's the high coroner, all for a buck-fifty per. In a bottle, or on something harder out of one of his hospital cabinets, he was always proud to sign whatever your old friend Dub put in front of him."

"Dub did the investigation, as sheriff?" I asked.

"Such as it was," Stud said.

"Well, why would the Readys want to kill themselves?" I asked.

"Now, your studship, you have stumbled upon the key-most question which we experts haven't been able to answer, up to this good hour," Stud Wampler said.

"Would there be somebody else who wanted to kill Hoyt?" I asked.

"Only six or seven hundred people in Vernon, maybe," Stud said. "Not to mention Wardell."

FIFTEEN

I think this bird's overwound his watch," I said to Stud Wampler. A highly nervous Doc Watson had suddenly excused himself and left us alone in his dinky little office in the basement of the Vernon Hospital, when we went to interview him a little after lunch on Tuesday. He'd said he had to go take care of an emergency and would be right back.

"His mainspring's about to pop," Stud said.

Watson had moved to Vernon after I'd left. So I'd never met him until that day, and I certainly wasn't overly impressed when I did. Wearing a doctor's white smock, about five-six with bushy black hair and Groucho Marx eyebrows, he'd come out to the front reception desk to receive us. His handshake was fleeting and weak, and he didn't look us in the eye. We followed him along a hallway, smelly with alcohol and other medicinal scents, then down concrete steps to his private office in the basement.

He hadn't sat down when we did, but had fidgeted for a minute or two, sweaty and shaky, standing just inside the office door. Then he'd suddenly taken off with his lame excuse.

We looked around. There was nothing the slight-est bit personal about the largely bare and tiny white-walled office—no family pictures, no plants, no books, no rug. Just Watson's framed osteopathic license on the wall behind a cold metal desk and chair and, facing the desk, the two additional metal chairs where we sat.

The only feature of the room and its contents worth giving a second glance to was a line of about two dozen spent bullet slugs along the front of Watson's desk. A small, hand-lettered tag was tied to each one. The slugs were arranged with compulsive neatness in a ruler-straight line, with each bullet the same quarter-inch distance from its neighbors and all of them carefully graduated according to size. Smaller .22 bullets were on the left end of the line, as we faced the front of the desk, larger .38s and .45 slugs on the right. Some bullets showed little dam-age. Others were flattened out in front or otherwise deformed by impact.

Doc Watson was true to his word and returned after only a few minutes, but he was transformed. He no longer seemed rushed or nervous. He was calm, almost languid, as he went around behind his desk and seated himself slowly. He put both his hands, palms down, on the desktop in front of him and looked up. Tranquil as he was, there was still something furtive, guilty, about him. The look in his eyes was like that of a kid who's done something wrong and is afraid you're going to find out about it.

"Well, I took care of the emergency situation," he said.

"What was it?" Stud asked, just to make Watson squirm.

"Nothing for y'all to worry over," Watson said, evasively. "So, now then, Sheriff, Mr. Wampler, in what way may I be of help to you?"

"Your coroner's report on Dub Ready," I said. "That's why we're here."

The lower right drawer of his desk was a file cabinet. He pulled it out, searched quickly, and took out a letter-sized tan manila folder.

"Here it is, the revised one," Doc Watson said, handing the thin file to me. "You need a copy? There's an extra there."

"Yeah, thanks," I said. I took out the copy and handed the folder back to Watson. I read the report quickly. It was a one-pager, back and front. "You want to amplify on this some?" I asked, looking up.

He opened the folder and took a minute to study the front and then the back of the original report. "I was misled at first, but this revised report is accurate," he said. "I shouldn't have put any stock in what the boy who brought in the body said."

Doc Watson glanced up to see how I was taking this. I returned his gaze, but didn't say anything. Maybe the reason he looked guilty, I thought, was because of his first, mistaken opinion about the way Dub was killed.

"Shot in the back twice, twenty-two-caliber bullets," Watson recited. "The higher one, probably the first, hit the bottom of his heart and then slammed into a rib and stayed there. That's where I found it when I examined the body, performed a partial autopsy." Doc Watson looked up from the report to the line of spent bullets on his desk. He picked up the first one on our left. Its nose was raggedly flattened. He looked briefly at the attached tag, then back at me. "This one, by itself, would have killed him. The second one went right through the body. The exit wound it made just below his left ribs looked almost exactly like a shotgun blast from the front."

He was trying to justify his first having called that exit wound a shotgun-shell entry wound.

Watson leaned forward to hand the slug to me. "It was a hollow-point, you can see. No live target is meant to survive that kind of bullet; it splays out on impact, as you know."

I took the slug from him. Sure enough, I could see what was left of the hole that had once been centered in the lead point of the bullet, now jaggedly flattened out where it had apparently hit the inside of one of Dub's ribs.

"You're right," I said, and handed the slug on to Stud. He looked at the bullet intently, then put it back in its place in the desk line.

"I'm surprised that he didn't die instantly," Doc Watson said. "The boy said he lived long enough to speak to you."

"He did, barely," I said. "He said something about taking care of Audrey and then Juanita."

"Something like that," Stud said.

"Here's the really curious thing," Doc Watson went on. He reached over and took three more tagged slugs from his collection line and held them out to me. I took them. All three were flattened in front. "These are the bullets I took from the bodies of Inez and Hoyt Ready two years ago, also twenty-two hollow-points, and they appear identical to the one I took out of Dub Ready's body."

I examined them, then showed them to Stud. "Like they was four of the Dionne quintuplets," he said. "Looks like they all might have been shot from the same twenty-two rifle."

"You did autopsies on the Readys?" I asked Doc Watson.

"Their bodies were badly burned," he said. "I'll go get the reports, if you want. Old reports are upstairs."

I said I *did* want. Watson left us alone in the office again.

"This time, may be our old friend, Mr. Hyde, that comes back," Stud said, talking like W.C. Fields.

It wasn't. Watson was still a calm Dr. Jekyll when he returned shortly with two more manila folders. Behind his desk again, he opened the folders and extracted the coroner's report each held.

"Here they are," he said, handing me one at a time. "This one's Inez Ready, and this one's Hoyt."

I took the reports. They were done on the same forms as the one for Dub Ready, the blanks filled out and comments noted in what I supposed was Watson's handwriting. I looked at Hoyt's file quickly, handed it on to Stud, then studied the report on Inez Ready.

"Both shot twice," I said. "But you've got just three slugs."

"Never found the second one that hit Mrs. Ready," Watson responded.

"Where did the bullets enter their bodies?" I asked. "You don't say in the reports. And which one died first?"

"Well, it was a double suicide. . . ."

"How did you decide that?" I asked. My tone was sharp. Doc Watson jerked his head up and looked at me. His eyes went wide.

"Well, everybody knew it," he said, looking away quickly. "The sheriff, Dub, knew it. Said so." The startled look on Watson's face that had appeared when I'd jolted him with my question was still there, but now he began to appear a little puzzled, too. It wasn't his earlier, guilty look. It occurred to me that he had just then realized that he could have made a mistake on the Ready couple's reports, the same way he'd first been mistaken about the cause of Dub's death.

"Stud, you never done no real autopsies on them bodies, did you?" Stud Wampler asked him. I looked over at Stud and nodded my agreement with his question.

"Well, not complete ones, no. Nobody thought we needed to."

"How'd you know that Miz Ready was shot twice, then?" I asked.

"Even burned as she was, I could tell that there was one entry wound and one exit wound in her left chest area, one entry wound in her back," Doc Watson said. "Probed down the entry wound in her chest and found the one bullet, that one there." He pointed to one of the three labeled slugs that Stud had put back on the desk. "No bullet in the other hole, the one from the back; it went clean through."

"So Miz Ready was obviously killed first, shot once in the front, once in the back," I said. "And Hoyt, how did he die?"

"Two slugs were in his chest cavity," Watson said. "I saw he was practically burned to a crisp in back, so I turned him over and opened up his chest. That's when I found the bullets that killed him, still there."

"You cut him open from the front?" Stud asked this before I could.

"Yes . . ." Doc Watson began hesitantly, already thinking ahead, obviously, to the next question.

"You didn't probe bullet entry wounds in Hoyt's chest?" I asked.

"It was a long time ago . . ." Watson said.

"Think!" I said. "Were there any entry wounds there?"

"Not in his chest—"

"—where you found the slugs," I said.

"That's right," Doc Watson said. He shook his head, puzzled. "That's right," he said again, this time more emphatically. "The only place he could have been shot—"

"—was in the back," Stud interrupted to finish

the sentence. "Shit for breakfast, man! You couldn't make a coroner in a Laurel and Hardy picture show!"

"If Hoyt was shot twice in the back, and Miz Ready was shot in the back *and* the front, it's damned sure that neither one of them shot the other," I said.

"My God!" Doc Watson said, the full impact of it all sinking in. He slumped forward in his chair, put his head in his hands for a moment, then looked up. "The Readys didn't commit double suicide," he said. "Somebody else killed them."

"What about a rifle?" I asked.

"Never found one, as I recall," Doc Watson said. "It was assumed to have been burned up in the fire."

"Now, if we could find *that* sucker, a twenty-two semiautomatic rifle," Stud said, "we'd probably know who killed all three of 'em—Dub and both his folks."

Doc Watson didn't rise when we did. He just sat, embarrassed, staring at us as we got up to leave. I certainly had no intention of saying thank you or shaking hands. I was disgusted with Watson. Stud and I started for the door. But then I thought of something else and turned back to face him.

"Yes?" he asked, apprehensive, the guilty look back again.

"What's paregoric got in it?" I said.

"Opium, anise oil, benzoic acid, and camphor." He recited this as if reading from a doctor's manual.

"Why are you giving it to Juanita?" I asked.

"I wouldn't say I'm giving—"

"—Selling, then," I said.

"Dispensing. It's for her nerves."

I said nothing, stepped back to the desk, scooped up the four tagged slugs I wanted, and put them in my jacket pocket. Stud and I got out of there.

Upstairs, headed down the hall for the front door, Stud muttered, "Dope fiend sonofabitch!"

I was about to agree with him when Audrey Ready called to me as we came even with the reception counter where she was writing in a file. I stopped and turned.

"Okie," she said. Putting down the file, she came out from the desk and tiptoed to give me a hug. "I was hoping to catch you."

She smelled good, looked good, too, in her white, well-starched nurse's uniform. I was glad to see her. I was a little surprised, though, that she was back at work so soon, two days after the funeral.

"No rest for the wicked," Audrey said by way of explanation. "Babies keep coming."

She said hello to Stud, then took me by the arm and began to walk with us toward the front door. Her forehead was wrinkled with worry.

"What's the matter?" I asked.

"Okie, I've got trouble I need to talk with you about," she said.

"What kind of trouble?" I asked.

"Got a woman back yonder about to deliver, so I can't go into it now," she said. We stopped just inside the door. "I had a bad scare, a threat really, this morning. Could you come by after I get off work this evening and tell me what you think I ought to do?"

"Can and will," I said.

"I'll cook a little supper for you," she said. We embraced again and said good-bye. She headed back down the hall.

"Who stood to gain from Hoyt Ready's murder?" I asked Stud, after we'd crawled back in the sheriff car outside and started toward the courthouse.

"Most crimes are based on greed or revenge," he

said. "I read that in a true detective magazine."

"Either one sound like enough motive for triple murders?" I asked.

"What does, stud?" Stud said.

We drove on back to the courthouse in silence.

SIXTEEN

Audrey was wiping away tears from her eyes with her apron hem when she opened the door. She started to cry again when she saw me, but quickly got control of herself.

"I'm sorry, Okie," she said, opening the front door to let me in. "I just can't get over it."

"Don't apologize," I said. I patted her on the shoulder. She turned and led me through the living room, back to the kitchen.

Audrey was the same kind of cook as my mother. So was nearly everybody else in Cash County. Mama had never used a recipe book—a dab of this, a cup or so of that, and "I hope I didn't forget and salt them butter beans twicet."

Most of Mama's recipes, if she'd ever written them down, would have probably started out with: "First, get the grease hot." All the meat we ate—home-cured ham and sausage, newly killed chicken, a meat-locker steak—was salted with a heavy hand and then fried nearly stiff. She salted and fried potatoes and mealed-okra, too, in plenty of lard. And Mama's string beans or a mess of greens always went into the pot with a good dose of bacon drippings that she'd saved in a tin can on top of the stove. Then, salted generously, too, they were boiled to kingdom come.

I loved that kind of down-home cooking, and Audrey knew it. She met me at the door that evening wearing a full, flowered apron over her housedress and led me back to the table in the kitchen. I put my Stetson on the counter by the telephone, pulled out a chair, and sat down at the rectangular oak breakfast table, taking the place set at the end nearest the dining-room door, as Audrey told me to.

She put out the food and poured herself some iced tea.

"You want buttermilk or sweet milk, Okie?" Audrey asked before sitting down herself. "I've got both in the Frigidaire." I took sweet. She poured it and took the chair to my left.

"Help yourself," she said. I began to. "But save some room for dessert."

There was both fried chicken and fried ham. Spinach and green beans that she'd canned herself from the garden, well-salted potatoes, mashed with butter and cream, and corn bread, hot out of the oven.

"Here's some pepper sauce for the spinach, if you want it," Audrey said, and passed me the glass bottle, stuffed tight with little chile peppers in vinegar. I shook out seven or eight drops of the clear liquid on the spinach, to tone it up a little, just the way I'd learned to like it at home.

"I'm worried, Okie, and I don't know who else to turn to," Audrey finally said. I'd been wondering when she'd get around to her problem, but I hadn't wanted to rush her. I looked up, chewing on a mouthful of good salty ham.

It was hot in the kitchen. Audrey wiped her face

with her white cloth napkin and pushed back a tight brown curl that had fallen over her forehead. She wore no makeup or mascara and no lipstick on her full lips, and I couldn't help noticing that she'd never lost that appearance of freshness and innocence she'd always had. But a scared and vulnerable look came into her dark eyes.

"What's happened?" I asked.

"When I came out of the house this morning to go to work, there was this guy waiting out in his car for me," Audrey said. "Mean-looking guy, dark-complected, one eye looking kinda off. Sharp clothes. He got out real quick and came over and grabbed me by the arm, before I could get in my car, and he asked me if I was Miz Ready. I brushed his hand off and said I was. He scared me. Gave me cold chills. Said he worked for Browney Greer at Lawton."

"Bootlegger that runs the Idle Hour Club on the south side."

"That's him," she said. "Said Dub owed Greer a big gambling debt, and the man wanted his money, right now."

"Say how much?"

"I hate to tell you. Nearly three thousand dollars. I told you I knew Dub was gambling up there—and losing, too. But three thousand dollars? Thug got ahold of my arm again, and this time he wouldn't let go. 'Listen, little lady,' he said, getting his gotch eye up close to my face. 'We're gonna give you three days, until Friday, to come up with the dough, all of it.' He said, 'Me and the boss'll be back this same time Friday morning, and you better have his money or you might not have them pretty looks no more.' He turned me loose, then, and I quick-like jumped into my car. But he caught the door and held it a minute, and said, 'And maybe we'll take some of it out in trade.' He rolled his eyes and laughed like the

Shadow, then slammed my door and walked off. I stuck it in reverse and was out of the drive and gone before he ever got in his car good."

"Don't worry," I said, hot. "I'll teach that gotch-eyed bastard a lesson, and Greer, too."

"You going to be waiting here for them Friday?"

"Naw," I said, "I don't want to put things off that long, and it's best to track outlaws to their own hide-out." I couldn't believe I'd said that. I sounded like Bob Steele in one of his B-movie Westerns. But I was mad as hell about the threat and the rude way Audrey'd been treated. I felt protective of her.

"I may be tied up tomorrow night," I said, "but we go up to the Idle Hour Club after they open Thursday night, you and me both. Make it look like we came to drink and dance, so they won't run off. You point out old Greer's messenger boy, and I'll clean his plow—and Greer's, too."

"Will you do that, Okie? Can you?" She reached over and took my left hand in both of hers. She still looked tiny and vulnerable, but less frightened.

"Sure, I will," I said. "I'm the sheriff."

Tears came to her eyes. I let her hold my hand a while longer before I finally picked up my fork with the other one and started in again on the mashed potatoes.

"I'm sorry, Okie," she said. She took back her hand and wiped her eyes with her apron tail.

"No need to be," I said.

"You think Browney Greer is behind what happened to Dub?" Audrey asked.

"Occurred to me," I said. "He is, you can bet we won't be long finding out. Hoyt Ready ever gamble, you think?"

"*Hoyt* Ready?"

"Yeah, Dub's old man."

"Not so far as I know. Why?"

"Just a thought, Audrey," I said. "Stud and I haven't told anybody else, but just this afternoon we found out that Hoyt and Inez Ready were murdered, too, and—"

"My heavens!" Audrey gasped, and put her hand up to her mouth. "Murdered? Who by?"

"Likely by whoever it was that shot Dub," I said.

"Who'd want to—"

"—Yeah, that's what we've just started trying to sort out. We don't know. But we'd just as soon the word about what we know—which, of course, isn't too much at this point—not get out right away to the killer, or killers."

"The Readys murdered, too," Audrey said. "What a mess!"

It was, and we both chewed on it in silence for a while with our food.

I finished eating a little after Audrey and handed her my plate when she got up. I'd forgotten what she'd said about dessert and was just about to crumble corn bread into my milk and eat it with a spoon, the way I'd done since I was a kid.

"Hold your taters, Okie," she said, and went over to a cake box on the kitchen counter and brought out a lemon cake with white icing, my favorite. She set the cake in the middle of the table, stuck a single candle on it, and quickly lit the candle with a kitchen match.

"Happy birthday, Okie," she said, then, and leaned over and kissed me lightly on the cheek. The date had practically slipped my mind. I blew out the candle, but I didn't make a wish. There were too many possibilities to choose from.

It was November 16, 1937. Oklahoma was thirty years old, and I was twenty-six. Neither one of us, I thought, had a whole lot to show for it.

SEVENTEEN

Wednesday, the seventeenth, was a clear and sunny mid-November day. The wind was blowing a little, as always in Oklahoma, but it wasn't too bad.

I'd shared a lot of what I knew with Audrey over supper the night before. But I'd figured that I wasn't obligated to tell her everything. I didn't tell her, for example, that Juanita was the reason why I'd said that I might be tied up the following night, Wednesday night.

It seemed like a month ago, though it had only been four days, that Juanita and I had agreed at the rabbit drive to go riding on Wednesday. And she'd called me at the sheriff's office the day before to say that she still wanted to stay with that commitment, even after everything that'd happened. She said that she'd meet me at the Billings place by about noon on Wednesday.

I got up early that morning and ran my usual two miles, the same as I'd done most mornings since high-school days. I always ran in heavy work shoes and sometimes carried short pipes filled with lead,

like I had when I was in training for boxing. My dad
thought I was nuts.

He was up when I got back to the house. We did
the regular chores, the same as always. We pumped
water for the stock and the chickens, caked the cows,
hayed the horses, gathered the eggs, milked, and carried in stove wood, coal oil for the cookstove, and
water for the kitchen. I caught up Badger, my little
gray quarter horse, curried him, then left him standing in the lot, a rope around his neck hitched to a corner post.

A little before eight, my dad and I took off separately. He was headed by Grandma Dunn's for coffee
and then on to the Vernon livestock auction. It was
held every Wednesday. My dad would be gone for
the night—to Oklahoma City with a load of cattle.

He looked weary as he left, and I was worried
about him. Sometime during the night, I'd been
awakened by one of his coughing fits, and I knew he
hadn't slept well. Maybe, I thought, a good slug of
the Echo Springs he kept in his old truck would
smooth him out a little and get him back on track.

I drove to the sheriff's office at the courthouse. It
was a cube of a limestone-and-concrete building that
hunkered squarely in the middle of a near-downtown
city block. As I approached the south door, I looked up
at the three-inch ledge that ran around the building at
the second-story level and grinned to myself as I
thought about my daredevil high-school days. After a
midnight movie at the Murray Theater, a bunch of us
boys used to come down to the courthouse, human-fly
our way up to that narrow ledge, then inch a precari-
ous tiptoed course on it, all the way around the building. The only more daredevilish thing we used to do
was to climb the Vernon water tower at night and
hang from the steel catwalk that girded it, a hundred
feet off the ground.

Nothing was happening at the sheriff's office Wednesday morning. Crystal was already there and had a pot of coffee perking on the hot plate in the corner. Stud came in with the breakfast trays for the two grain-theft prisoners upstairs. He'd picked the food up from Irma, down at the Truckers Cafe. She had the county contract.

"We fight crime and/or evil," Stud said in his W.C. Fields voice, by way of greeting as he entered. He set the trays down on a desk and went over and poured himself some coffee. Turning, he held the mug up toward Crystal and me, as if making a toast. "And this is our weapon," he said. "We'll scald the bastards!"

Crystal and I opened the metal door and climbed up the interior stairs with the trays to feed the two prisoners. We cleaned their cell while we were up there.

Back downstairs, she showed me how to fill out the State Crime Bureau referral form for the comparison of the four .22-caliber slugs. She packaged them up and went to the Mistletoe Express office on the corner to send them off.

After Crystal got back, she and I and Stud mostly just sat around, killing time. I knew we ought to be doing something more about the triple Ready murders. But what?

Finally, a little before noon, I stood up, and said, "Bad crime wave breaks out, y'all handle it on your own." I got my mackinaw and Stetson.

"Done sleuthin' for the day, are you, stud?" Stud said to me.

"Different approach," I said. "Adding things up. Deducing. Waiting for a break. All the good crime fighters do that." I headed off to the Billings place.

Juanita was already there when I got back. She was unloading the strawberry-roan mare she called

Sugar from the rear of the metal, two-horse trailer
that she'd pulled behind her Jimmy pickup.

She was dressed in khaki poplin-twill slacks and
rawhide boots. The rounded collars of a cotton
blouse, white as her perfect complexion without
makeup, showed outside the high neck of her beige-
wool sweater. Over it, she was wearing a brown-
suede jacket that came down to her hips. The sun
made a sheen on the long black hair cascading down
in back from under a lady's narrow-brim, dark
brown Stetson.

"Thought maybe you'd had a memory lapse,
Okie," Juanita said, as I got out and walked over.
"Or a change of heart."

"Neither one," I said. "The law's a jealous mis-
tress."

"Me, too," she said, killing me with the tease in
those green eyes. She gave me Sugar's reins and
slipped on a pair of brown-suede gloves that she
took from her jacket pocket. She picked up her tan-
leather purse from the ground near the back of the
trailer and slipped the long strap over her head,
hanging it from her left shoulder and under her
right arm.

I handed her back the reins and gave her a peck
on the lips. Even that fleeting physical contact was
electric for me, and I turned away at once, so that
she wouldn't see the quick flush that I knew must be
obvious, even on my suntanned face.

It didn't take any time for me to get Badger sad-
dled up. He hadn't been ridden for a few days, and
he tried to pitch a couple of times when I got on him,
but I wouldn't allow it. My dad had taught me that.
"Don't never let a young horse buck on you, or a
coonhound trail armadillos," he always said. "Rerns
'em."

Juanita put her left boot in the stirrup and swung her lithe body easily up on the roan. Our ponies were impatient to get going. We turned them loose and went out to the section-line lane in front of the Billings place, rode a half mile east to the corner, then headed south on the bus-route gravel road— through flat and gently rolling wheat and cotton fields and native-grass pastures on each side. Off to our left, a half to three-quarters of a mile and paralleling our route, was the gray-dark north–south line of the thick East Cash Creek woods, mostly native pecan, oak, elm, and hackberry.

"The boys want to cook dinner for you," I said to Juanita after a while. "Saw them in town yesterday."

"Your uncles?"

"Yeah, they've got a crush on you," I said.

"About my speed, those two," Juanita said with a wry smile. Then, her mood, and tone, turned dark. "But I'm glad somebody likes me. I'm so alone, now, Okie, except for you. You sure Dub was murdered, like you said on the phone the night before the funeral? That it wasn't an accidental shooting?"

"No question, I'm afraid," I said. I couldn't bring myself to add, right then, that we'd also learned that her folks hadn't committed suicide, either. She had enough to worry about, I thought.

"First, my folks die," she said. "Now, somebody kills Dub. You think we'll ever find out who? And what if I'm next? What if they're after me, now?"

"I feel sorry for you, Juanita," I said. I really meant it. "But don't worry. Nothing's going to happen to *you*. I'll see to that. And we'll find the killer. You can count on it." I hoped I sounded more confident than I felt. Still, I did have a line of investigation in mind, and it was one reason behind the ride to see my uncles.

Juanita and I switched away, then, from talking further about Dub's death. Like most people did at funerals after a few words of condolence, we pretty quickly got on to happier thoughts. We fell into a kind of laughing nostalgia about old times as our horses stepped rhythmically along.

"What about that Thanksgiving Thursday," I said, "when I crowned you Turkey Queen at halftime in the Vernon-Wardell football game, and I tripped when I went to kiss you, and we both fell over backward out of the wagon?"

Then it was Juanita's turn. "Remember how bad we were when we put on *Richard III*?"she said. "Made the drama club sponsor, Miz Gooch, sorry she'd ever moved to Vernon."

"I killed off about half our class in that play," I said.

"And remember how Miz Gooch said your humpback was good, but that you didn't have to drag around like the Mummy in that Boris Karloff picture? Being from back East, she said that your performance was the first time she'd ever known that King Richard had an Okie accent: 'Naow is the winner uv ar discontint.'"

Juanita's laugh sounded good. I hadn't heard it since I'd come home. Dub's death was a terrible thing. And there'd been some bad intervening years, especially for Juanita, after we'd both left Vernon. But I began to hope that all that was behind us, that we might take up where we'd left off and make a fresh start.

Two miles south from where we'd turned, we saw old man Nahnahpwa, the Comanche, ahead on the road in front of his home-allotment land. The Comanche tribe had no fixed reservation. That'd been broken up by the government in 1901. Tribal members had been scattered onto checkerboard,

160-acre allotments around the area, and white people had been permitted to settle on the rest of the Comanches' old lands.

Nahnahpwa sat on his bay pony bareback in faded blue overalls and a worn navy pea jacket while he grazed about a dozen mixed-breed mother cows on the tall, dry buffalo grass in the right of way alongside the road. Long gray braids hung down from under the wool navy watch cap he wore. There was no readable expression on his completely hairless brown face as he watched us ride closer.

The old man nodded at me as we came nearly up to him. He wouldn't look at Juanita. *"Hah, mahdu-ahwe,"* he said to me in Comanche, by way of greeting.

"Hah, tsa nuh nuisikite uh puhneets," I responded.

The old man switched to Spanish. That didn't surprise me. He knew something of that tongue because his father had been a white Comanche captive as a boy and had retained a lot of his native Spanish. I'd taken some Spanish in high school, and Nahnahpwa had always liked to talk a little of it with me when he'd had the chance.

"Tú montas caballo hermoso," the old man said as we'd come even with him.

"Si, señor, lo robé," I said. The old man laughed.

"Ten cuidado! No montes a la hermosa," he said then. We both laughed. *"Y muchas gracias por enviar a los muchachos para limpiarme la charca."*

"De nada," I said. Juanita and I rode on.

"What was all that, Okie?" she asked, after we were on down the road a ways.

"He just said hello in Comanche, and I said it was good to see him. Then he said in Spanish that I was riding a good-looking horse, and I said I'd stolen it."

"And what did he say after that, when you both laughed?"

"He said 'Be careful, don't ride the pretty one.' Could be taken two ways."

"He doesn't like me," Juanita said. "Dub tell you about the oil on that old man's land?"

"Yeah, the old man just thanked me, too, for getting Marsh Traynor to send his boys to clean the pond they dumped mud in when they drilled the test well. But I don't know if Audrey's going ahead with Dub's oil deal or not—in Dub's place. Haven't asked her."

"Why wouldn't she?" Juanita said. "Big payday in the leases Dub already had, whether you drill them or sell them. Good money to be made by somebody."

"Dub said so," I said.

"That's another one that doesn't like me—Audrey."

"Why would you say that?" I said.

"She's always been a little resentful of me, I think, Okie," Juanita said. "The last year or so, Dub's been running around on her and gambling, and she thinks I encouraged all that."

"Did you?"

"Well, I went with him, some, to Lawton, if that's what you mean, and she doesn't like that. And, as a matter of fact, I think she's always been a little jealous about me and you, too—and probably is, now."

"You're wrong about that," I said.

Juanita looked over at me and smiled teasingly, raising her eyebrows. "I wouldn't blame her, if she is jealous."

In a little while, we came to my uncles' barbedwire gate on the east side of the road. I got off and opened it, led my horse through, waited for Juanita's mare to pass in, then put the gate back up.

Before I could remount, my uncles' hounds

started bawling. The old ramshackle, tin-roofed house was a good two hundred yards away, down two deep ruts cut through the close-cropped pasture that was dotted with mesquites. The house was backed up against the heavy woods of East Cash Creek. But the three coonhounds—one a bluetick and the other two, black-and-tans—had caught sight or scent of us quickly, and they started loping toward us, baying in chorus.

Right behind the hounds came Uncle Joe Ray and Uncle Leroy. Slat-slim and trotting, too, they were almost baying, themselves, their shouted, excited words tumbling over each other.

"Tol' ya that uz them, tol' ya!"

"Hit *is* them! Hit *is* them!"

"Tol' ya that uz them, tol' ya!"

The hounds got to us first. They saw it was me and quit bawling and began to circle us, jumping excitedly, tails flopping every which way in greeting. The horses shied a little, nervous. Uncle Joe Ray and Uncle Leroy soon got to us, too, and they were just as worked up as the dogs.

You might have thought the two of them were twins, except Uncle Leroy's face was slightly puffier. They both wore ragged, wool army trousers and shabby, high-top work shoes with no socks. The army trousers, like the uncles' scarred, shell-shocked psyches, were artifacts of their unbearable dough-boy service in the hellhole trenches of the Great War.

Uncle Joe Ray had on a gray-cotton shirt, out at the elbows, Uncle Leroy, no shirt at all, only a dingy undershirt, even though the weather was cool. Neither one of them had shaved lately, and their rough old faces were covered with gray stubble. Both were bareheaded, and it looked like they'd recently taken turns cutting each other's wild gray hair and had pretty much botched the job. Their twang and east Texas way of talking reminded me of my mother, their sister.

"Tol' Leroy that uz you-uns, soon's I heared them dern dogs commence to take on," Uncle Joe Ray said, cackling and showing his snaggle teeth— stained brown, what there was left of them. He came around on my right side and reached up and took my gloved hand. "How you, hon?" he said.

I said I was fine.

"Shootfar, I knowed it was you-uns, my ownself," Uncle Leroy said. He went around on the other side and took Juanita's left hand. "How you, pretty lady?" he said.

We made for the house like that, Juanita and I on horseback, my uncles on each side of us in a kind of jog, holding our hands. The two of them talked all the way, and the three hounds kept running and cir-cling the whole bunch of us.

"Made you-uns squirrel dumplin's, the likes you ain't never eat," Uncle Joe Ray said, snuff juice drip-ping out of the slack right corner of his mouth.

"Kilt 'em this morning in the woods, four of 'em," Uncle Leroy said. "Acourse, they old boars. Won't be no young-uns 'til spring."

I interrupted. "How come you're not wearing a shirt, Uncle Leroy?" I asked.

"He's awarshin' it," Uncle Joe Ray answered for him.

"I'm awarshin' it," Uncle Leroy said. "I am." He grinned. His teeth were no better than his brother's, and they were equally brown with snuff juice.

"Best to cook them old boar squirrels with dumplin's," Uncle Joe Ray went on. "Too tough to fry. Acourse, ye gotta cut their manhoods out quick, soon's ye skin 'em. Don't, them glands gonna make they meat too gamy."

At the unpainted and weathered old four-room shack, the hounds went up under the fatigued front porch. The uncles let go our hands.

"Get off, you-uns," Uncle Joe Ray said to Juanita and me.

"Yeah, get off and come in," Uncle Leroy said.

Juanita and I dismounted and tied our horses to a porch post that was none too stable.

"Hope the horses don't do a Samson on us," I said under my breath.

"Me, too," Juanita said.

The uncles ushered us in the front door. "Make yourselfs to home," Uncle Joe Ray said. But there was no way we could do that in the room we entered, the front room. There was no available space left. Except for a narrow aisle that led from the front door and the bedroom door to its right, back to the kitchen, the room was piled nearly shoulder high with stacks and stacks of musty old newspapers and magazines, tied into bundles with binder twine. There was an upright piano in one corner of the room, but you couldn't have gotten to it because of the stacks.

I'd seen all this before, but Juanita was stunned.

"How long have you been collecting this stuff?" she asked.

"Let's see, pert near eighteen year, ain't that right, Leroy?" Uncle Joe Ray said.

"Why do you keep it?" she asked.

The uncles both giggled, as if that was a funny question.

"They's *so* many good things in ever'one of them papers and magazines," Uncle Joe Ray said in explanation of what he plainly thought was the obvious.

"Ol' lady Beech at the beauty parlor always saves the *Colliers* and *Sat'dy Evenin' Post*s fer us," Uncle Leroy said. "And we git leftover *Vernon Herald*s at the paper and the *Lawton Morning Press* at the drug-store, sometimes two or three copies of each one."

"Take a look at air one of 'em," Uncle Joe Ray said. He picked a bundle at random and, bringing his pocketknife out from a pants pocket, cut the twine that bound it and shook the dust from a maga-zine on top. "Fer an example, lookie at this here *Colliers*."

We did. It was from June 1930. Seven years old.

Uncle Joe Ray opened the magazine to an interior page and pointed a bony finger at one of the pictures there. "That there's old Hoover a-fly-fishin'," he said. "Too bad he didn't just keep on a-fishin', 'stead of bein' president. Not a bad man. Engineer, though, no training in guvmint. Didn't know shit from a good grade apple butter about the economy, neither. Let us git into this here Depression."

"That there's Mama and Papa, in that pitcher," Uncle Leroy interrupted, changing the subject and pointing a bony finger at a dark photograph in an oval frame on the north wall. He turned away, then leaned over a stack of papers and picked up an object from a half-hidden table behind the stack. Blowing the dust from what appeared to be a painted-chalk model of a hot-air balloon, he said, "This here's from the St. Louis World's Fair. Aunt Rose give it to us. Hit's a balloon, and people go up in the real thing, too. We seen it in the war, ain't that right, Joe Ray?"

"That's right," Uncle Joe Ray said. "Now, let's go git sumpn d'eat. Won't take no time to set the table."

When we got through the stacks to the kitchen, Juanita excused herself to go to the outhouse, carry-ing her leather purse with her. I drew out one of the unpainted beechwood chairs and sat down at the rickety old pine table. My uncles started setting it with plates, bowls, spoons and forks, and coffee cups. No two of anything matched.

Uncle Leroy took the lid off a blackened pot on the wood cookstove. A rich vapor swirled out. He carried the pot over and placed it in the middle of the table. With a giant wooden ladle, he began to fill the bowls with the steaming squirrel and dumplings.

"You-uns gonna like this," he said.

The three of us delayed eating for the couple of minutes or so it would take for Juanita to return. I used the time to bring up a question that was on my mind.

"So, ya'll got a new gun, you told me yesterday?" I said. This was my new line of investigation. Riding to my uncles' place, I was stoning two birds at once, as my dad would have said. "You shot these squirrels with it, I guess."

"Joe Ray left the cleanin' waddin' in the barrel of our old long Tom, and hit plumb blowed up on us," Uncle Leroy said. He'd forgotten that he'd already told me that, the day before.

"Marsh Traynor," Uncle Joe Ray said. "Comes down here huntin' a right smart. Left us his own twenty-two rifle last Sunday. Knowed we needed it."

"He didn't come down here last Saturday, then?" I asked. "It was the next day, Sunday, right?"

"Hit sure were, were Sunday, didn't come Saturday," Uncle Leroy said. "He said he didn't need that twenty-two. Said fer us to just keep it long's we-uns wanted. Left us a box of hollow-point cotridges, even. Dern good guy, old Traynor."

"There it stands, there in the corner," Uncle Joe Ray said.

Twenty-two rifle. Hollow-point bullets. Brought it Sunday, the day after Dub was killed at the rabbit drive. And if Marsh Traynor wasn't at the rabbit drive on Saturday, I asked myself, where was he that particular morning?

I got up and went over and took up the rifle. It was a semiautomatic and looked old and well used.

"Ya'll mind if I trade guns with you for a week or so?" I said. "I need a twenty-two for a little while. I could drive down tomorrow morning, early, and bring you my four-ten and pick up this one."

I'd already made a plan in my mind that I'd Mistletoe Express the Traynor rifle, like I had the four Ready .22 slugs we'd gotten from Doc Watson, to the state crime lab in Oklahoma City for testing. I didn't want to be thinking along those lines—Marsh Traynor was close to my dad, and I liked him, too—but I knew I had no choice. I had to try to find out whether, as I feared, the bullets that killed the three Readys had been fired by Traynor's rifle.

"Good deal, Okie!" Uncle Joe Ray said. "My eyes ain't what they was. Four-ten'd be a sight better for huntin' squirrels."

I set the gun down and went back to the table. Juanita returned. We all started in on the squirrel and dumplings, and I was glad that Juanita seemed to like the spicy meal as well as I did.

The uncles chattered away like a couple of courting squirrels, themselves, talking mostly to Juanita, whom they were clearly taken with.

We all cleaned out our bowls, and Juanita and I took some stout coffee with the uncles and then said our good-byes. They were reluctant to let us go and walked halfway up to the gate with us.

She and I got back to the Billings place a little before the sun went down. We tied our horses by the back door and went into the house. I made myself some iced tea and opened a bottle of Progress beer from the icebox for Juanita. We sat down at the dining-room table. I switched on the floor-model Philco radio. It was powered by a car battery that was hidden in the bottom of its wooden cabinet and that we had to hook up to one of our trucks and recharge periodically. Through the radio's static, the mellow voice of Bing Crosby soon came crooning, "When the blue of the night meets the gold of the day . . ."

"Juanita, you want to go to the picture show tonight?" I asked. "It's *Love under Fire* with Loretta Young."

"Got a better idea," she said, crinkling her nose mischievously. "Think we might start us a fire here?"

"We could try rubbing a few things together and see," I said.

EIGHTEEN

The dark and smoky Idle Hour Club on Lawton's south side was beginning to get loud and lively when Audrey and I arrived there at around nine o'clock on Thursday night.

In Vernon, she'd cried when she'd first got into the blue sheriff car, said it reminded her of Dub. But, after that, we'd driven the narrow concrete slab of a highway to Lawton, five miles west and seventeen north of Vernon, without saying a whole lot. I'd parked the sheriff car on a side street about a block away from the nightclub. It was situated in a made-over ranch-style house that was bookended on either side by a Texaco station and the Comanche Teepee Tourist Cabins.

A hard-looking woman checked our coats and my cowboy hat at the door and led us back to a toy table against the north wall of the crowded main room. It was a room that had obviously been made by knocking out a couple of interior walls in the former residence.

Our table was in a good spot to give us a clear view of the hall across the way, which I knew from

Cameron College visits led past a gambling room and on back to Browney Greer's office.

I'd left my badge in the car on purpose. I was dressed like a civilian, with an open-necked white shirt, a blue-and-gray sport jacket, and gray gabardine slacks. Audrey looked great in a long, navy, pleated skirt and middy blouse.

A three-piece band banged out a Western swing number over the background clink of glasses and bottles and the low roar and clamor of customers trying too hard to have a good time. The nightclub's tables were filled. A good number of the customers were uniformed soldiers from nearby Fort Sill.

A bartender in a soiled white apron quickly appeared to take our totally illegal cocktail orders and wipe off the tabletop with a wet rag. I asked him for a salty dog—gin, grapefruit juice, and lots of salt. It was about the only mixed drink whose name I knew. Audrey ordered a manhattan.

The drinks came quickly. We took a few sips and continued to look the place over. The band ended one song and then, with hardly a pause, began another, this one "Blue Moon."

"Might as well dance," I said.

"Might as well," Audrey said. I led her toward the crowded little dance area in front of the dinky corner bandstand. Years had slipped by since the two of us had danced together, and I'd forgotten how tiny she'd feel in my arms. She was wearing pumps; but still, her carefully waved, short brown hair barely came up to my shoulders.

When the number ended, she and I began to edge our way back through the tables toward our own. In mid-passage, we both at the same time suddenly caught sight of the swarthy gotch-eyed guy we were looking for as he emerged from a door at the end of the long hallway on the south side of the room. He was wearing a loose, yellowish Hawaiian shirt, and he spotted us, too, the minute he turned from the door.

We stopped. So did he. It was obvious that he'd recognized Audrey, equally apparent that he knew she'd recognized him.

Audrey didn't have to tell me that this was the same thug who'd threatened her in Vernon. I knew it from her quick intake of breath and the suddenly tight grip of her hand on mine. The guy's own surprised look was a dead giveaway, too.

That look of his swiftly turned into a scowl, then he wheeled and went back into the room he'd come out of, slamming the door rapidly behind him.

"Come on!" I said to Audrey. I took her hand. We hurried through the tables to the hallway and started down it, passing on our right the open door of the gambling room, where a crap game and a card game were in progress at two different tables. With Audrey right next to me as we reached the end of the hall, I twisted the knob on the door and roughly shoved it open. In doing so, I practically knocked down old Gotch-eye, who'd been standing just inside.

Our sudden entrance unnerved Browney Greer, a fat man with slicked-down hair parted in the middle. Eyes big, he lurched up from his chair behind a little wooden desk on the other side of the small wallpapered room. A bare lightbulb hung from the middle of the ceiling. A dishwater blond babe who'd been seated on a worn leather couch to Greer's right jumped up, too.

Gotch-eye, about my height, but thirty pounds heavier, quickly regained his balance in the middle of the room, where the door had pushed him, and he whirled around toward us. He took a big step forward and gave me a hard shove in the chest with his right hand and at the same time, with his left, reached behind to his belt in back, under his shirt, and pulled out a heavy, murderous-looking .45 automatic pistol and started to swing the business end of it around in my direction.

Audrey yelled. I dropped my hand from hers. I vise-gripped Gotch-eye's left wrist with my left, leaned forward to push the gun downward as a deafening shot from its barrel exploded into the linoleum floor, and then, on instinct, crashed a solid overhand right straight into the thug's sharp nose. I felt the cartilage crack as the blow hit home. My dad always said, "Make your first lick a good-un." I had.

Gotch-eye grunted hard, dropped the gun to the floor, and staggered back into the dishwater blonde. She screamed, and the two of them tumbled together onto the couch, the woman sitting down hard, the man sprawled across her, sideways. Blood streamed between the fingers of the hand that he'd brought up to his nose, and large scarlet drops splashed onto the front of the woman's unstylish pink-silk dress. She began at once to squirm, trying to get out from under him and push him off.

Outside, the music and noise had stopped when the shot went off, and people were stalking down the hallway toward us to see what had happened. Greer came out from behind his desk and brushed past Audrey and me to the open door.

"No problem, folks," he said to the gathering onlookers in the hall. "Go on, now. No problem."

He stepped back inside the room, where the acrid cordite smell from the gunshot remained heavy in the air. He closed the door and started back for the safety of his desk. My ears were still ringing.

"Get off me," the blonde said to Gotch-eye as Greer moved past her. The thug got to his feet shakily and took out a handkerchief from his back pocket. He held it to his still-flowing nose, and the blood quickly began to soak through the white cloth.

Gotch-eye squared himself to confront me, glowering menacingly over the reddening handkerchief. "You broke my goddamn nose, you sonofabitch!" he said. In Oklahoma, people got killed for calling somebody a sonofabitch in anger.

"I meant to," I said. I took a step forward and kicked him in the crotch as hard as I could. He let out a dreadful groan and fell to the floor in a ball, his face purple. I picked up the .45 from the floor and stuck it in the front of my belt. I stepped back beside Audrey. She made no sound, but took my hand again.

The blonde slid herself farther over to the end of the couch, away from me, a scared look on her washed-out face.

"Who are you?" Browney Greer asked. He was standing behind the desk, steadying himself on it with his hands. His face was shiny with sweat.

"I'm somebody you're gonna be damned sorry you ever messed with, Greer, you and that shit, there," I said, nodding toward Gotch-eye, who was trying to get up. My voice, a low growl, sounded as angry as I felt. "What's his name?"

"Otho Parks," Greer said.

"I'm the law, now, in Cash County, that's who I am," I said. "Either one of you set foot there again, or ever say so much as another word to Miz Ready, here, the ex-sheriff's widow, and I'm gonna put you so far behind bars they'll have to pipe sunlight to you." Audrey moved closer to me. "You know what I'm talking about, Greer?" I said.

"Yes," he said, and sat down heavily in the desk chair, a look of resignation on his face. "I do."

"And what about old Otho there," I said, motioning. "He understand it, too?"

"Same for him," Greer said. "Ready owed me a lot

a money I'm losin'. So'd his sister, that Juanita. This deal don't cover her."

"Sure as hell does!" I said this with authority, taking care not to show surprise at hearing for the first time that Juanita also owed gambling debts to Greer. "We came about *both* of them," I went on. "You're not gonna collect on either one of those debts. Forget that. Gambling's still against the law in Oklahoma."

"No shit?" Greer said sarcastically. "Just got out of two weeks in the Comanche County jail. Sheriff here makes a little show for the church crowd. Then he's right back for his monthly." He curled his lip and made a money motion, rubbing his right thumb and forefinger together.

"Well, I'm not," I said. "Were you in jail on Saturday, the thirteenth of this month, then?" That was the day that Dub was killed.

"Yeah, guest of the county," Greer said.

"What about him?" I said, nodding toward Otho Gotch-eye, who still stood glaring at me. His nose had stopped bleeding, and he was holding the handkerchief down at his side.

"In there with me," Greer said.

Audrey and I moved together, back toward the door. I put my hand on the knob, but kept my eyes on everybody. "You don't want to mess with me or Miz Ready, here, ever again—or the ex-sheriff's sister, Juanita, either," I said. "You get that?"

"We get it," Greer said. He said it like he meant it.

"See that you don't forget," I said sternly, and started to turn the doorknob.

"Juanita comes back, though," Greer said, "they ain't no deal on her."

"Give me back my piece," Gotch-eye said.

"Like hell," I said. "I've got a guy that can use this in our fight against crime and/or evil."

Audrey and I left, and I closed the door behind us.

The hallway was empty. As we passed in front of the gamblers' door, men stopped their card and dice play and eyed us with curiosity. In the big room, the music had started up again, but people at the tables watched us cross through to the entrance. The hatcheck woman gave us our things in silence. I left her no tip.

Neither Audrey nor I said anything until after we were in the car and on the highway to Vernon.

"My lord, Okie, you knocked the tar out of that thug," Audrey said.

"Without thinking," I said. "Same thing that got me in trouble up at Norman."

"You in trouble at the university?"

"Hit a law professor," I said.

"Not recommended," Audrey said.

"Me and him got in an argument in the hall over what he'd said in class against President Roosevelt."

"Have to hit him, though, for that?"

"Not for that," I said. "For putting his hands on me. I've always had this weird thing about that, can't stand it. Doesn't make sense, but I can't help it. The professor made the mistake of grabbing hold of my shoulder, and I just automatically slapped him before I thought. I didn't want to hit him. Might have hurt him. But I'm sorry to say that I still rattled him pretty good. It wasn't smart, and I was immediately sorry."

"What'd they do?" she asked.

"Kicked me out. I apologized and appealed to the student disciplinary committee. We had a hearing. But they still haven't made a decision."

"Go back, if they rule in your favor?" Audrey asked.

"Expect so," I said. "But about tonight, we learned something. I'll check on it, but if Greer and old Gotch-eye were in jail Saturday the thirteenth, like

Greer said, we have to say they didn't shoot Dub."

"True," Audrey said. "And then we're no closer to finding the guilty ones than we were. But I'm so much obliged to you, Okie. I mean it. I don't think Greer or his gun-thug'll try to bother me anymore."

"You know Juanita was gambling that much herself?" I asked.

"About what I figured," Audrey said. "She always seems to be almost desperate for money, and maybe that's part of the reason. She's so changeable, too, sometimes nice, sometimes real hateful, almost like—and I hate to say this—she's on something."

"I know old Doc Watson's selling her paregoric," I said. "I wish she wouldn't take it."

"Might be selling her something worse," Audrey said. "That's what I've been afraid of. Another reason, maybe, why she's been so hard up for money."

"What else might Doc Watson be selling her?" I asked.

"He may be on morphine himself," she said. "There's too much of it coming in and out of the hospital just to be for medicinal purposes. I'm the only one who's got a key to the case besides him, and I know *I'm* not taking it."

"I find out he's selling Juanita, or anybody else, morphine, I'll run his osteopathic ass out of town," I said.

"If she's on that stuff, it would be hard to get her off of it," Audrey said. "I think, now, that the times she seemed the most hateful to me and Dub was when she might have been needing a shot. The worst time was over Dub's oil deal that he wouldn't let her in on."

"I hope that's not true," I said. "We've got to help her. What're you going to do about that oil deal?"

"Well, I have the leases that Dub got and paid a lot for. My thought is that I should sell them outright

to somebody, maybe Marsh Traynor, and not try to
farm them out for drilling, like Dub was going to do.
What do you think?"

"Sounds reasonable," I said. "Make some money.
Less risk. What about old man Nahnahpwa and his
family's allotments? I'd promised Dub I'd try to get
leases on them for him."

"We ought to go ahead with that, if you'll help
me."

"Stud and I are going to the Waurika sale tomorrow, but let's you and me drive down and see old
man Nahnahpwa Saturday afternoon," I said. "He'll
sign up, I think, if I can talk to him. Why wouldn't
he?"

NINETEEN

Friday was the weekly livestock-sale day at Waurika, the little town twenty miles southeast of Vernon, close to Red River. Stud and I rode down there together in my Chevy truck, my dad separately in his own. The sale barn was on the blacktop highway at the west edge of town. It was a two-story frame building with wood siding and a corrugated-tin roof and was nearly surrounded by about a quarter of a city block of cow lots.

I'd skipped my running that morning. Instead, I'd gone, early, down to my uncles' place, picked up Marsh Traynor's semiautomatic .22 rifle, and brought it back for Crystal to Mistletoe to the Crime Bureau in Oklahoma City.

Still, that left enough time so that, by ten that morning, Stud and I and my dad were in the front row of the two dozen seats that were reserved for cow-trader regulars, just inside the dirt-floored half-moon cockpit of the Waurika sale ring. Up behind us was the small amphitheater of stepped wooden bleacher benches where about fifty farmers, occasional bidders, and spectators were gathering.

"Okie, I cain't believe you're right about him," my dad said when we'd settled into our chairs and I told him about sending Marsh Traynor's rifle to the Crime Bureau. "I'm ashamed you done that."

"We'll see," I said.

The sale auctioneer was Art Murdoch. He carried the title of "colonel," like all auctioneers, and followed an unchanging weekly livestock-sale circuit—to Duncan on Monday, Lawton on Tuesday, Vernon on Wednesday, Wardell on Thursday, and Waurika on Friday. Murdoch was a good guy, basically, always dressed like a prosperous rancher, and he was known as something of a ladies' man.

The colonel stepped self-consciously up the four steps to the raised counter in front of the ring and sized up the traders and the crowd. He took off his black hat and hung it carefully on a nail. He sat down next to the woman clerk and said something to her that caused her to blush. Then he swallowed a mouthful of water from a glass canning jar on the counter and banged his gavel hard, announcing that he was ready to sell the first group, three head of fed steers, that had already been let into the ring from the outdoor cow lots.

"All right, now, boys, let's weigh 'em," he said in the deep bass voice that he worked like a musical instrument—meaning that he wanted to sell the steers by the hundredweight, rather than by the head. "And what're you gonna give for 'em by the hundred?" He launched, then, into the auctioneer's sale singsong and filler babble.

Two old cowboy-looking guys, one called Shorty, the other Junior, began to shuffle around in the dirt ring, now and then loudly popping long hard-handled whips to bunch and turn the three steers and show them off. Shorty and Junior's job was to take bids from the buyers and pass them on to the auctioneer.

The two of them focused intently on first one prospective bidder and then another, sometimes pointing at a trader with a whip end until they got the quick nod or quiet finger signal they wanted.

"Yeah!" Shorty shouted, when he took a bid, and the auctioneer ratcheted the hundredweight price up a notch and continued.

"You're out, over here," the auctioneer stopped to holler, pointing to the earlier bidder with his gavel, then resumed the cry at the higher figure.

"Yeah!" Junior yelled, signaling a raise from a different cow trader. The auctioneer upped the price again.

I loved the grand mixture of cattle-auction sounds—the rhythmic and staccato cry of the auctioneer, the shouted outbursts and whip cracks of the helpers, the occasional bawling of the cattle.

I loved the good-natured, but competitive, banter of the cow-trader fraternity, the tingly atmosphere of excitement and financial risk that pervaded the ring, and the secretive bidding by the buyers.

I loved the smells—the bitter cow odor of the sale ring and the sharp and greasy, combined scents of mustard, pickles, onions, and frying hamburger meat that wafted out from the adjacent makeshift café under the same big roof.

I'd known all of this from my earliest years, riding to sales with my dad.

That morning in Waurika, Stud and I were partnered up, and I did the bidding for both of us, with him rasping a whispered word of advice in my ear now and then. Sitting next to my dad and knowing his ways, I was careful not to jump in when he was bidding. He did the same with me, so that we wouldn't compete with each other.

I started bidding right away on the first lot of steers. The competition for them from the other buyers was heavy, and the price went up fast. But I stayed in.

"All done? All through?" the auctioneer called out at last, his eyes searching the faces of the traders and those in the first farmers' rows, while the two helpers, too, queried with raised eyebrows the individual traders they were working.

"Sold to Okie Dunn, right down here," the auctioneer announced then. He pointed the gavel at me, then banged it down on the counter. I'd bought the three steers—worth the money, I thought. Junior took the sale slip, handed down from the counter by the woman clerk, and brought it over to me.

That was the way the morning went. My dad and I alternated our bidding until, by the time Colonel Murdoch announced a brief recess for lunch, Stud and I had already bought a bobtail truckload of cattle. My dad had, too.

The three of us got up and stretched, as the other cow traders did, then went out of the arena into the cement-floored space in front of the café counter. We got in line and bought three hamburgers, two NeHi oranges for Stud and me, and a Coca-Cola for my dad. Stud and I moved back into the center of the area and bunched up with the others of the crowd who were gathered loosely there around a potbellied woodstove. It gave off some welcome heat against the coolness that hung under the high, tin-roofed ceiling.

My dad handed his hamburger to me to hold for him and stumped off to go to his truck, carrying the Coke. When he rejoined us after a while, I was not surprised to see that what had been the bottle's dark brown liquid had paled to amber. Poured out some Coke and filled the bottle back up with Echo Springs, I figured.

My dad looked weary, and he was breathing unnaturally hard. He was sweating, too, and his face was redder than usual. I knew that he'd made more than one trip out to his truck that morning. But he still seemed to be in good enough shape to buy cattle and drive to Oklahoma City with a load.

"No good sonofabitch!" my dad suddenly said under his breath. I was standing right next to him. He and I and Stud were finishing off our burgers.

"What?" I said.

"I didn't say anything," my dad said.

He was staring hostilely past the stove at a man on the opposite side of the room, and the man was glaring back at my dad with matching anger in his dark eyes. Tall as Stud and just about as solidly built, the man was black-headed and maybe five years younger than Stud, ten years younger than my dad. He wore the work uniform of a Progress Beer truck driver and route salesman—blue-and-white-striped coveralls with the familiar circular red trademark on the back. The man curled his lips, said something angrily to my dad that couldn't be heard, then wheeled and left out through a side door without looking back.

"Who's that?" I asked.

"Chickenshit 'bout to git his ass whupped," my dad said.

I knew not to ask again. We threw our bottles and used napkins into the topless oil drum set up to the side of the stove for garbage.

A cattle trucker named Ray Gene Ritter sidled over to us. He was a little curly-headed guy with a humpback and a houseful of kids. He had a run-down old International ton-and-a-half truck, and I knew he needed work. "Y'all still lookin' for some-body to haul your load a cattle up to the City?" he asked me and Stud.

I said we were and pulled the sale slips out of my shirt pocket.

"Let's go over here to the office, and Stud and I'll pay out and give you the bill of sale," I told Ritter. "You're to take the load to Ralph O. Wright. That's the commission house we use at the stockyards."

Stud and I and Ritter swiveled around toward the office. My dad turned in the opposite direction.

"See you birds in another tree," he said.

"Where you headed?" I asked.

"Gotta see a man about a dog," my dad said enigmatically, and hobbled off toward the side door on his gimp leg.

My partner and I and the trucker started for the office.

I don't know whether I had a premonition or not. Maybe I was just worried that my dad might make one trip too many to his Echo Springs stash and get too drunk to drive. Whichever, I felt a twinge of apprehension as we separated from him.

There was business to attend to, and it took us a while. Stud divided up the sales tickets, so that each of us would pay about half the total purchase price of the cattle we'd bought that morning. He and I wrote out separate checks and gave them to the older of the two women who were clerking the sale. The bill of sale she made out and handed us, and we passed on to Ray Gene Ritter, identified our cattle by the numbers on the paper tags that had been glued on the right rumps of each one when the Waurika sale had taken them in. We reminded the trucker again of which commission house to take the cattle to and where to find us in Vernon for his pay when he came back from Oklahoma City with our check and the receipt.

"Y'all spare somethin' in advance for gas?" Ritter asked. I gave him three dollars.

Stud and I didn't figure on buying anything else. We'd already put together our load. But we went

back to the sale ring again, anyway, for want of anything better to do, and took our seats. My dad wasn't
back. His seat was empty. Stud and I joshed for a few
minutes with the other cow traders on each side of
us.

A rank brindle bull was let into the ring for the
start of the afternoon session, and Colonel Murdoch
banged the gavel a couple of times for order. He was
just beginning his spiel again, when the younger of
the two women who worked in the office suddenly
leaned down from behind me and touched me on
the right shoulder to get my attention.

"Okie," she said in a low, but distressed voice,
getting her mouth close to my ear as I turned
around, "Hudge is out there in a bad fistfight! I'm
afraid he's gonna get hurt."

Stud and I bounded out of the ring to startled
looks, rapidly crossed the open space in front of the
café, and slammed through the exit door. Off to our
right about twenty yards, as we came outside, down
by the loading chutes, we saw a bunch of shouting
onlookers, ringed around two men fighting in the
graveled parking area.

It was my dad and the Progress beer truck driver,
and they'd obviously been going at each other for
some time. Stud and I got there just in time to see my
dad take a crushing fist to his left ribs. It knocked the
breath out of him. He staggered backward and sat
down hard, then began to cough violently while he
squeezed his side protectively with his left arm.
There was blood on his lips and a mean cut on his
forehead. Both his cheekbones were badly swollen. I
ran and knelt beside him, and when I did, he
grabbed my arm for support and struggled up to his
knees. But he was still racked by terrible coughing,
and his breath came in loud wheezes in between the
spasms. It was clear that he'd taken an ugly beating.

"Stay down," I said, and stood up, myself, facing the driver of the beer truck. He'd backed off a couple of yards or so and was a little shaky himself. There was a badly skinned place as big as a silver dollar on his right cheek, his nose was bleeding, and his lower lip was swollen fat. But he was still mean and belligerent. His red eyes were hot, and the huge fists at his sides were clenched hard. He focused on me.

"You want some of this, do you, sonny?" he said angrily.

"Listen," I said, "this is all over. Get on out of here, and we'll drop it, for now."

Behind me, my dad had stopped coughing and had made it to his feet. I looked back and saw him suddenly whip his pocketknife out of his right pants pocket and quickly unsheathe its main blade.

"I'm agonna cut you a new-un," he said around me to the truck driver.

"Get that old man out of here, boy," the truck driver said to me, "or I'm gonna make him *eat* that knife." He didn't back up.

Just then, Stud stepped up and grabbed my dad in a bear hug from the back, pinning my dad's arms at his sides.

"Come on, Hudge," Stud said soothingly, and held him tightly. "There's gonna be another time." My dad struggled, but he couldn't get loose. He started coughing again.

I turned back to the big truck driver, and we glared at each other. "Get on out of here," I said.

"You the one that's gonna git out of here," he said. "You don't, I'm gonna whip *your* ass."

"Hope you brought your supper," I said deliberately. "May take you a while."

He suddenly lurched forward and shot a big right fist at my head. I bobbed and took the lick on my left shoulder. It shook me, but I steadied myself, took a half step forward, and dug a hard left hook into his stomach, just above the belt line. In the same motion, I wrapped the left on up and around and jarred it solidly to his right jaw. He staggered a second and stepped backward. But he didn't go down. Instead, he let out a roar and swung a killer roundhouse right that just barely missed my chin, as I bobbed, on instinct, and he followed the right with an equally wild left. I bobbed again, and his fist, big as an Osage orange, struck me glancingly on the right side of the top of my head. It felt like a sledgehammer had hit me, and my knees buckled.

The big truck driver must have busted a knuckle on my head with that blow because he didn't immediately follow up. Instead, he hesitated a beat and a half, and I took advantage of it. I caught him with a stiff left jab to the nose that raised his chin up, then set both my feet in the gravel and slugged him with a right cross to the jaw that had my whole 147 pounds in it. I felt the jolt up my arm. He started down, and I struck him with a mean left hook to the right temple as he fell. He was out when he hit the ground. In fact, hitting the ground seemed to bring him to a little, but not enough so that he could get up right away.

It was over.

TWENTY

My dad was pretty groggy when Stud and I loaded him in my truck for the trip back to Vernon, and both his eyes were nearly swollen shut. He didn't resist or protest. His breathing was wheezy, and he coughed intermittently, groaning when he did. He held his left ribs protectively with his arm as we got him up in the truck seat on the passenger side.

We closed the door behind him and walked back around to my side of the truck. I told Stud that I was going to take my dad to Doc Watson's in Vernon. We both knew that something was badly wrong with him. Stud said that he'd settle up my dad's cattle purchases and drive his truck back. I asked him to go by Grandma Dunn's when he got to Vernon and bring her down to the hospital. I got in, started up, and headed onto the highway.

"What's between you and that beer guy?" I asked after a while.

My dad coughed and held his ribs, but didn't say anything for a minute or two. When he did speak, he didn't look over at me, but kept his head down.

"Well," he said finally, in a low and groaning,

kind of ashamed, voice, "me and him been playin'
the same ol' gal."

"Old Irma?" I said. "Piss-poor reason!"

My dad didn't respond, and we drove on for a
time in silence. He dropped his head again and, after
that, only straightened up every now and then when
he was racked by another coughing fit. His breathing never got easy during the whole trip.

"How long you been coughin' up blood?" I asked
him after one coughing spell.

"Blood and corruption, two or three months," he
said. "And hit seems like I'm always wore-out."

When we finally entered the outskirts of Vernon
from the south, my dad roused up a little and
noticed through slitted eyes that I'd kept going on
through Snuff Ridge toward downtown, not turning
east on South Boundary toward the Billings place.

"Where you fixin' to carry me?" he asked.

"I want Doc Watson to take a look at you," I said.

"I wouldn't let that sumbitch work on one of my
calves," my dad said. The exertion caused him to
start coughing again, and he held his ribs and
groaned as he did so.

"Not aiming to have him *castrate* you," I said,
"though that might not be such a bad idea. I want
him to see about that coughing and 'tend to your
ribs."

I thought I'd get more fight out of him when I
said that, but I didn't. He closed his eyes again,
resigned.

After Doc Watson examined him in the emergency room and x-rayed him and fixed him up
some, Audrey wheelchaired my dad back to a hospital room where I'd been told to wait. Stud and
Grandma Dunn had already joined me there. Stud
and I stood nervously against a wall. Grandma sat in
the only chair.

The cut on my dad's forehead had been stitched and bandaged. A spot of brown-red iodine had leaked through the white gauze. One of his eyes was totally shut, the other just a slit. His features were distorted, his face lumpy and bruised.

He still had on his scuffed cowboy boots and dirty Levi's. He was wearing the same gray work shirt, the tail out and loose. His Stetson and brown coat were in his lap.

Audrey said a brief hello to us and bent down and folded up the footrests of the wheelchair, so that my dad could get out. She picked up his hat and coat and took one of his arms. I moved quickly to take the other. We helped him up and steadied him as he hobbled a few steps and sat down heavily on the side of the hospital bed with a groan. Audrey crossed and hung his jacket and hat on a hook on the far wall.

"You want us to take your boots off, Mr. Dunn, so you can lie down?" she asked him solicitously as she came back to the bed. She spoke a little louder than usual, as if to a deaf man.

My dad's voice was weak, but he still had some fight in him. "Tol' ya I weren't takin' them boots off," he said. "I'll lay down, but I sure'n hell ain't stayin'."

We helped him bring his legs around and stretch out on the bed, with the knee up on his bad leg. Audrey fixed the pillow so that he could get his head comfortable. But he'd no more than lain down before another coughing fit hit him. Audrey gave me a look of concern and cranked him up in the bed to something more of a sitting position. That seemed to help. She handed him a tissue and stood by the bed, holding his hand until the coughing subsided. Then she went back and stationed herself by the open door.

"Doctor will be down to talk with y'all in a moment," she said. I didn't like the sound of that. I felt a little sick at my stomach.

"How are you, Miz Dunn?" Audrey said to Grandma, who was still sitting.

"I was doin' all right 'til this here hit," Grandma said, nodding toward my dad. "Weren't no time to change clothes. I'd jes come back from cleanin' house for Miz Mildren, Methodist preacher's wife."

Grandma got up then and went over and stood by the bed. She was wearing a cotton dress with a blue work apron over it and heavy, black, low-heeled shoes with strings. Her thin white hair was pulled back severely from her pinched face and fixed in the usual bun.

"How ya doin', son?" she asked my dad. He opened the only eye he could a little, and there was a brief flash of vulnerability, perhaps of fear, in his face when he looked up at her. I'd never seen anything like that from my dad before. It gave me a deepening feeling of dread.

"Tolable, Ma," he rasped, and closed his one good eye again, breathing with effort.

Doc Watson, in a white smock, a stethoscope around his neck, came in brusquely and strode over to the bed, all business, not acknowledging the presence of any of the rest of us. The short Groucho Marx look-alike with bushy black hair seemed to be in one of his calmer moods, I noted. He spoke directly to my dad, with no sugaring up of the bad news.

"Mr. Dunn, you've got lung cancer," he said in a formal tone of voice. "It's in both lungs. The ribs—two of them on your left side—are cracked. Nothing we can do about that. Can't bind them up. Breathing would be too shallow. Your cancer, Mr. Dunn, is well advanced. It's going to get pretty rough for you, I'm afraid."

"Already is," my dad wheezed. "Is it gonna kill me?"

"Yes," Doc Watson said, simply.

"How long?" my dad asked in a low voice. "Should I be plantin' any fruit trees?" He managed a crooked smile.

"I don't believe I would," the doctor said, humorlessly.

"What about settin' a hen, then?" my dad asked. "Time for that, at least?"

"Close case, I'm afraid," Doc Watson said. "We can keep you as comfortable as possible here."

At that, my dad rolled on his side and, leaning on his left hand, sat completely up, grimacing as he did so. He swung his legs around then until they were hanging off the side of the bed.

"Take me home, Okie," he said to me, and slid off to his feet, wincing as he did so and resting one hand on the bed for support. "Ain't nair one a my people ever died in no hospital. Gimme my coat and hat."

I did. He put the hat on gingerly over his bandage. I helped him on with his coat, trying not to hurt his ribs too much.

"Suit yourself," Doc Watson said.

"I am," my dad said. He limped unevenly toward the open door, breathing heavily as he did so. Stud moved quickly to take his arm. Grandma Dunn got up and followed them. I held back a moment with Audrey and Doc Watson.

"Thanks, Audrey," I said.

"I'm sure sorry, Okie," she said.

"How long's he got?" I asked the doctor.

"Days or weeks, at most," he said. I anticipated that answer, but my heart sank farther, anyway. "Pretty far gone. The fact that he can't clear his lungs well because of the broken ribs will make it quicker and worse. It's going to be really bad for him.

Probably pneumonia. Lots of pain."

"I don't aim for him to hurt," I said, making Doc Watson look me in the eye. "I want Audrey to give him as much painkiller as he needs, and whenever he needs it. That clear?"

"Too much could hasten his death," Doc Watson said. "And the law's strict on that."

"You're the last one I want talking to me about the law!" I said harshly. "You're going to hear from me about that, too. But, right now, just do it!"

"All right," he said.

At the Billings place, Stud and I moved the table from the dining room into the living room. Then we brought in a daybed and put it where the table had been and shoved the table against the south wall.

The dining room was the central room of the house and the only one with heat. The potbellied woodstove sat toward the west side of the room on a circular metal pad laid on the linoleumed floor. The south-corner door to the kitchen and the west one leading to the two bedrooms could all be shut to keep the room warm.

A norther had started blowing. Stud and I tacked up a thick old quilt, one of many that Mama had made, over the open archway between the dining room and the living room, which was on the north side of it. My folks had always improvised that kind of insulation every winter, after the weather had turned cold, to hold the heat in the dining room, where they stayed most of the time.

Grandma Dunn got my dad as comfortable as possible in the bed, after he'd taken off his boots and clothes in his bedroom and put on some green-flannel Christmas-gift pajamas, which I knew he hated. She brewed him some coffee, and the heat of it seemed to help him. He grew still, though his breathing was labored, and soon went to sleep.

Stud left for the sheriff's office. Grandma and I got ourselves some coffee and came back and sat down near the stove.

"Nothin' to do but pray, now, Okie," she said. "Only the Lord can hep him." I knew she was right. We sat in silence.

After a time, Grandma spoke again. She surprised me by putting a question to me on an unexpectedly different subject. "You still goin' with that Juanita Ready, Okie?" she asked.

"I am, Grandma," I said, and automatically steeled myself for what I anticipated would be an unpleasant commentary about Juanita. Grandma surprised me again.

"Well, she's a good girl, to my mind," Grandma said.

"She is, Grandma," I said. "She's gone through some rough times. I hope I can help her get back on her feet."

"I do, too," Grandma said. "You know Miz Mildren keeps poor people's kids down in the Methodist Church basement, so their mothers can work at the WPA sewin' room. And she tol' me that Juanita comes and heps her fer nothin', and she shore 'preciates it. Hardly ever misses a day, she says.

"Says pore Juanita never had no chance, growin' up, the way her dad done her, ol' Hoyt Ready," Grandma Dunn said.

"How do you mean?" I asked.

"Messed with her, poor thing," Grandma said, "'til the girl finally couldn't put up with it no longer and tol' her brother, and they both moved off to town. And Inez—this here's, to me, just as bad as what ol' Hoyt done, might neart—Inez to all appearances knowed right along what was happening and never said nary a word 'til after the girl and her brother had up and left home."

"I never heard anything like that," I said, deeply shocked. Juanita abused by her own father? "Juanita, or Dub, either, never said a thing. How did Miz Mildren find out?"

"Mustn't never tell this nor let on you know it," Grandma said, "but Miz Mildren once tol' me that Hoyt and Inez come to the parsonage of an evenin', years ago, right after Juanita and her brother moved out on their own to town, and ol' Hoyt looked like a suck-egg dog and cried and confessed the whole thing to Brother Mildren. And he and the Readys prayed a right smart together, and ol' Hoyt finally got right with the Lord and swore up and down he'd never be guilty of doin' nothin' like that again. Inez cried and prayed over it, too. And they both asked Brother Mildren to try and talk the kids into comin' home. But the kids never done it."

Now I knew why Dub and Juanita had moved to Vernon to finish high school and why both of them had ever since felt hard toward their folks.

TWENTY-ONE

Saturday morning, I awoke at five, as usual, and took my morning run. Back home, I washed up and put on my Levi's and plaid flannel shirt as it started getting light. Grandma Dunn was already up, of course. She was in the kitchen, whistling "The Old Rugged Cross" and making breakfast. Grandma'd agreed to move in with us for a while to help take care of my dad. He was up, too, but still in his pajamas and socks, a clear sign that he was in bad shape.

My dad was sitting in a rocking chair near the hot woodstove, drinking coffee and smoking. His face was still badly swollen. I sat down in a straight-backed chair next to him to pull on my boots.

"How you makin' it?" I said.

"Tolable," my dad said, dangling a Camel cigarette from dry and cracked lips that looked a little purplish, like he wasn't getting enough oxygen. He took a shallow drag on the smoke and went immediately into an obviously painful spasm of coughing, holding his left ribs with a protective arm. I gave him a look of worry and, probably, disapproval, but I didn't say anything.

"Too damn late to quit now." My dad rasped out the answer to the question I hadn't asked, at least out loud. He was right to say that, I figured.

"Ad on the radio says, 'I'd walk a mile for a Camel,'" he went on, between coughs. "Dern truth is, you smoke enough of them Camels, and you *cain't* walk." I thought to myself that he was right about that, too.

I milked the cow and did all the other chores at the Billings place by myself, bringing in, last, several armloads of split-oak stove wood. At the kitchen table, Grandma laid out the kind of breakfast she'd once cooked for fieldhands. I scarfed up home-cured sausage patties and two eggs, sunny-side up, then sliced open two of her hot soda biscuits, and ate one of them after pouring good and salty white gravy, made with bacon grease, flour, and milk, over its two halves. I buttered the other one and covered it with thick, ribbon-cane syrup that had been part of a load my dad had hauled from Mississippi when he'd last visited the kinfolks back there. I washed everything down with a glass of icebox-cold sweet milk, passing up Grandma's stout coffee, figuring I'd wait to get a cup at the sheriff's office.

I thanked Grandma Dunn for the breakfast and for helping out with my dad. I touched my dad on the shoulder and told him to take care, then drove to the courthouse.

Crystal was already on the job, of course, and her usual, illogically sunny, self. Her thin, scrubbed face was as cheerful as the faded cotton dress that hung loosely on her long and gawky frame was pathetic. She had the coffeepot perking on the hot plate in the corner.

Stud came in with the prisoner trays from the Truckers Cafe and an extra one for Crystal. I knew she wasn't getting enough to eat at home, so I'd told

Stud to start bringing some food for her, too. Crystal thanked him and sat down at her desk at once to eat. The scrambled eggs, bacon, and toast weren't much, but it was pretty clear from the way she ate them that they were more than she was used to.

While Crystal finished her breakfast, Stud and I went upstairs to feed the prisoners—the two Randlett men charged with grain theft and a Vernon boy who'd been caught two nights before by the Vernon night watchman as the boy was trying to break into the back of Clif's Jewelry on Main Street.

We cleaned out the cells and came back downstairs. I closed and barred the heavy metal door to the jail. Crystal had put away her empty breakfast tray. She handed Stud and me two hot mugs of coffee.

"Deputy Pilkington called from Wardell while y'all was up in the jail," she said. "Had a killin' last night at Poss Tatums's joint. Some white guy stabbed another'n in a card game. Stabbee's here at Stigler-Martin funeral parlor. Stabber's locked up at the Wardell city jail. Deputy wants y'all to come down and pick up the prisoner, if you can. Says his old truck's broke down, or he'd bring the guy his-self."

"Call Pilkington back, Crystal," I said, "and tell him Stud and I'll come by his feed store and get him about ten and go to the jail together."

The deputy ran a little hole-in-the-wall feed and livestock-supply store on the south end of Wardell. He had a large family to provide for and helped to make ends meet by peddling a little hay, a few doses of worming and pink-eye medicine, and occasional bottles of rat and predator poison.

I was glad to have a reason to go down to Wardell. The killing in Poss Tatums's place would, I thought, give me the chance to press Tatums harder to tell me the name of the Vernon businessman that

he and Dub Ready had framed on the deviant sex
charge. I'd been rolling around in my mind a hunch
about who that man was.

Stud and I finished our coffee and drove three
blocks south on Church Street to the funeral home.
The skinny Slade boy, who worked there after school
and on weekends, said Greg Martin was on a hearse
run to Devol to pick up the body of an old lady
who'd died in her sleep. The Slade boy took us to the
lab room and showed us the body of the man who'd
been killed in Wardell. Two deep stab wounds, one
in the stomach, one in the chest.

"Call Doc Watson and tell him to come over here
and make out a coroner's report," I said to the boy.
He replaced the sheet. The three of us started back
toward the front of the funeral home.

"You might tell the good doctor, my boy," Stud
said in his W.C. Fields voice, "that the deceased was
run over by a steamroller and see how long it takes
him to figure out different."

"Huh?" The Slade boy looked at Stud quizzically.

"Forget it, son," I said. Stud and I went out to the
sheriff car at the curb and took off for Wardell.

Deputy Pilkington, a wiry little guy with a .38 on
his hip and handcuffs hanging on his cowboy belt in
back, was waiting for us out front at the little frame
building, a shack on south Main in Wardell that was
the headquarters for his modest feed and supply
business. A few busted bales of alfalfa hay lay this
way and that under a high tin awning on the north
side of the building. Pilkington padlocked the front
door and came over and got in the backseat of the
sheriff car.

"Looks like you 'bout outta hay," Stud said to the
deputy after we'd said hello to each other, and I'd
put the car in gear and started toward the jail.

"Sold all I had, not quite two weeks ago,"

Pilkington said. "To Dub's sister, Juanita, matter of fact—she's been a good customer to me. I ain't been able to git any more in here, on account of the drouth in south Texas."

"What'd you get for it—the hay?" Stud asked. "Been needin' some myself."

"That there good alfalfa, Juanita give me four bits a bale, and I stacked it in her barn, the other side of Essaquahnahdale," Pilkington said. "Took me two trips to haul it out there on my old bobtail truck. Took her some salt blocks for her old cattle, too, and a couple of bottles of strychnine she wanted. They always baitin' coyotes out that way. Left the blocks and poison in the old harness room in her barn. She wasn't there. And she ain't paid me yet, neither, and I could sure use the money."

"You get any more hay in, I'd take a load at that price," Stud said. Pilkington said he'd let Stud know.

I pulled up in front of the small redbrick jail building that hunkered in the shadow of the town water tower on the west side of Wardell. The three of us got out. Pilkington picked out a shiny skeleton key from a key ring that he pulled out of a pocket of his Levi jacket and opened the wooden front door. We stepped into the narrow corridor between the door and a big iron-barred cage that took up nearly all of the interior space in the little building. A rusty woodstove squatted in one corner, but there was no fire in it, and the place was cold.

"Cold as a well digger's ass in here," the prisoner, a big man, around forty, complained as he raised up. He was lying on a low bunk against the far wall.

"So's the guy you stuck the knife in last night," I said.

The man kicked off a flimsy, blue-and-white-striped cotton blanket and got up stiffly, fully clothed. He was wearing Levi's and boots and a wool jacket. His eyes were red and puffy, his face blotched.

Pilkington opened the cell door with a big iron key from the ring he held. The man—his name was Sid Bone—picked up his cowboy hat from the jail floor, slapped it against his leg, and put it on.

"Loan us your cuffs," I said to Pilkington.

The deputy took them from his belt and handed them to me. He fished out a small key on a little chain from his pants pocket and passed that to me, too. The prisoner put his hands behind him when I told him to, and I snapped the handcuffs on. We walked him out and put him in the backseat of the sheriff car.

Pilkington handed me the crumpled brown-paper bag he'd picked up from the jail-building floor, just inside the front door. "Right here's the knife Bone done it with," he said.

I took the bag and passed it on to Stud. He got in the passenger seat. I climbed in under the wheel. Pilkington slid in with the prisoner, and I drove back and dropped him off at his store. Then I turned the car toward Wardell's east side.

Poss Tatums's beer joint was on the corner of two dirt streets in the middle of the town's Negro residential section. It was a two-story, once green frame house with an unlit neon Progress beer sign in one of its windows and a poorly hand-painted metal sign on the corner that identified it as the Southern Club. Behind the bar building, at the back of the same lot, was a smaller, somewhat better-kept, house with yellow siding where I knew Poss lived. The two buildings were connected by a long, covered walkway.

I parked on the side street by the smaller house. Stud stayed in the car to watch the prisoner, and I crossed a ditch and stepped up on the small porch at the back of the house. I knocked on the screen door. There was no immediate response from inside. I hammered on the screen door with my fist.

"Poss, you in there?" I said loudly. "Open up." I banged again.

The inside door opened a little. Poss stood there in droopy white longhandles and socks. He rubbed his eyes.

"Well, 'at you, Mr. Sheriff?" he said. "Hold whatcha got a minute. Be out dreckly, soon's I git my overhalls on."

He closed the door. I stood there for a while in the chilly shade, and I was close to banging on the door a second time when it finally opened again. Poss appeared, pulling a single blue-overall suspender over his shoulder and latching it as he did. He'd put on a floppy, brown-felt hat, but his uncombed, nappy hair stuck out of it on each side. His lower face was covered with the white stubble of unshaved whiskers that framed the bare scar on the side of his chin.

Tatums closed the wooden door behind him and let the screen door bang to. He followed me off the porch, where there wasn't room for both of us, to the brown Bermuda grass of the small yard.

"What's the deal on this Bone guy?" I asked.

"He a mean drunk, Sheriff," Tatums said. "Playin' poker. Thank that other white dude cheatin', jump up and whip out his frogsticker all suddenly, and punch holes in him. Then, jes' slumps back down in his seat. Practic'ly done passed out when that deputy I call git heah. All she wrote."

"He doesn't plead, you're gonna have to testify," I said.

"Yassuh."

"And another thing," I said sternly.

"Yassuh, what that be?" He looked me in the face

for the first time. His eyeballs were yellowish, the same as when I'd seen him at the county jail.

"I'm gonna give you a choice," I said. "Either I close your ass down, slap a padlock on that beer joint of yours, right now, or you tell me who the Vernon man was that you and Sheriff Ready framed on that deviant sex charge. One or the other."

"Don't wanna tell that, Sheriff," he said quietly, still looking me in the eye. "Man kill me. Went to his house, other night, call him out, so his wife don't hear, and 'polagize to 'im. Old Poss plumb sorry he ever got in such a mess. Never do nothin' like 'at agin. Still, man kill me, I tell you his name."

"Take your choice," I said. "You'd rather I close you down, I'll damn sure do it."

"Don't want that neither, Sheriff," Tatums said.

"What about this, then?" I said. "What if I say a name, and if it's the right one, you just nod? Won't have to say a word."

He studied about the proposition for a while.

"Go ahead on, then," he said, finally. "Got ol' Poss 'tween a rock and a hard place, heah, look like."

"Marsh Traynor," I said. Poss Tatums's eyes went wide. This wasn't a wild guess on my part. I'd been thinking, ever since I'd sent his .22 rifle to Oklahoma City for testing, that Traynor might be the white man that Dub had framed. He'd told me at the funeral that Dub and his chief deputy Merkle had been trying to shake him down.

I knew, too, from when we'd first talked at his bank, that Traynor'd held a hard grudge against Dub. The frame-up could have been the reason. And that grudge could have been plenty of motive for Dub's murder. I knew that I, myself, might have killed somebody for a thing like Dub had done to Traynor.

Poss Tatums looked away. Then, slowly and almost

imperceptibly, he nodded. I was right about the name.

"Marsh Traynor, then," I said. He didn't say anything. I pivoted to go back to the car, then turned back to face Tatums again.

"I may close you down yet, if you don't clean up your operation here," I said. I didn't know what I meant by that.

"Yassuh," Poss said.

I went, then, and got into the car, and Stud and I headed back to the courthouse in Vernon with our prisoner.

"I was right," I said to Stud after we hit the gravel highway. "Marsh Traynor, that's who they put the frame on. It looks, more and more, like all we have to do is wait for the report to come back from the State Crime Bureau on Traynor's gun."

My dad had warned me, all right, when I took the sheriff job, that I'd probably wind up having to arrest close friends.

"Okie, my boy," Stud said in his W.C. Fields voice, "we might do well to remember what your old daddy always says and not come down with a bad case of the eagers."

Stud was right, of course. We had to wait for the final piece of proof to come in. But there didn't seem much doubt about which way the string of evidence was pointing. Still, I had the feeling that I'd heard some discordant snippet of fact that morning that didn't fit—something, it seemed to me, that Deputy Pilkington had said. But as we drove along toward Vernon, I couldn't for the life of me recall exactly what that troublesome fact had been, though I figured it would come back to me in time.

TWENTY-TWO

That afternoon about two, I went over in the sheriff car to Audrey's house, across from the courthouse, to pick her up. She was expecting me and came out as soon as I pulled into the driveway. Her usual black-and-red nurse carpetbag bounced on a wide strap over her right shoulder as she tripped down the front steps.

She hurried around to the passenger side, opened the door, and pitched the carpetbag in the seat, before sliding in after it. Closing the door, she turned back and patted me on the shoulder in greeting. Then, for a moment, she teared up again on being in Dub's car and, just as quickly, apologized for it, dabbed at her eyes with a small handkerchief, and soon became her bright and cheerful self once more.

We drove southwest, through town and past the Billings place, and then turned farther south on the main gravel road. After a couple of miles on it, we came to the barbed-wire gate, on the east side, that led to old man Nahnahpwa's place, down next to East Cash Creek.

When the Comanche Indians' big southwest

Oklahoma reservation had been broken up in 1901, and members of the tribe were forced to choose individual, quarter-section tracts before the rest of the land was divided among white settlers by lottery, some Comanches, like old man Nahnahpwa and his main family members, had been lucky enough to get to make early selections. They chose black bottom-land parcels near a creek, instead of having to take the kind of red-dirt and slick-hill dryland tracts that made up so much of Cash County. The good Indian lease that my Uncle Joe Ray and Uncle Leroy lived on, farther south, belonged to one of the old man's sisters.

I got out to open Nahnahpwa's gate, leaving the car motor running. Audrey slid over and drove through and then moved back to the passenger side. I closed the gate and crawled back under the wheel.

"Old man Nahnahpwa had an all-night peyote ceremony last night," I said as I put the car in gear and we started bumping down the rutted road through the pasture. It was about a quarter of a mile east to the frame house, and we could see, next to it in the yard, a tall canvas tipi with a couple of feet of circled, thin pole tops jutting out at the flap, with blowing strips of red cloth tied to a couple of them. "I woke up about five this morning, and I could hear the drum, still going strong," I said. "Sound carries. I hope the old man's up by now."

We pulled into the bare-dirt area in front of the white frame house, and I killed the motor. Two brick pillars held up the roof of the long front porch, and low green junipers flanked the concrete steps that led up to it. A mixed-breed dog, maybe partly coyote from his appearance, loped out from the red barn on the east side of the house. He bared his teeth and growled menacingly as he circled the car, but then retreated to the east side of the porch and eyed us warily from there with yellow eyes.

The tipi on the west side of the house, its flap-closed entryway facing east, was quiet. So was the house. We waited in the car.

After about two or three minutes, the front door opened, and Lucy, Nahnahpwa's wife, came out, drying her hands on the folded white-cotton cloth that was wrapped tightly around her waist—a *peet-squeena*, they called it. She wore a light blue butter-fly-sleeved cotton print dress that was cut like a tra-ditional buckskin shift and came down nearly to her beaded leather moccasins. The old lady stepped halfway down the porch stairs.

"Get off, y'all, and come in," she said as she stopped, speaking in Indian-accented English. She pushed back some loose strands of tightly braided gray hair from her brown and deeply wrinkled fore-head.

Audrey left her nurse bag in the car. We got out and walked to the porch.

"How are you?" I asked, and shook Lucy's out-stretched hand. "This is my friend, Audrey."

"Yeah, I know you," Lucy said, shaking hands with her, too. "You work at the hospital."

"That's right," Audrey said. "Glad to see you."

Lucy turned and led us up the steps and into the house. "Old man'll be out in a little bit," she said. "Peyote meeting here last night. Sit down, y'all." She motioned toward the faded wine divan facing the iron stove in the middle of the room, where a good fire was going. We seated ourselves.

"I'll get you some coffee," she said. "Y'all want pecans in it?"

I said we did, and the old woman went out to the kitchen.

Dark, oval-framed photographs of relatives hung on all four of the smoke-grayed walls, which had long ago been covered with a once off-white wall-paper that featured an endless design of small, crossed red rosebuds. A low table against one win-dow held a blown-up and framed high-school picture of the old couple's youngest son, Marvin. He was the one who'd been killed in a car wreck, and he'd been my friend, though the two of us were also fierce boxing competitors.

The old woman came back in a little while and handed us the two cups. We thanked her. Shelled pecan halves floated in the strong coffee, and there were spoons in both cups to eat them with. Lucy set-tled down to our left on a wine, stuffed chair that matched in both color and wear the couch where Audrey and I were. She and I sipped our coffee and ate the pecans. Lucy sat quietly, her weathered brown hands in her lap.

Pretty soon, old man Nahnahpwa came in from a bedroom, and Lucy immediately got up and went to get coffee for him. He was wearing black-and-white-striped overalls, a gray work shirt with a red necker-chief, and black high-top shoes. The old man'd apparently taken time to fix himself up for us. He looked pretty fresh, too, not like he'd been up all night, singing and praying with other peyote-road followers. His well-brushed gray hair was neatly divided into two long braids, each intertwined and tied with blue yarn. His brown face was, as always, plucked clean of all hair. Silver peyote-bird earrings dangled from each of his long earlobes. The part in the middle of his hair had been reddened, and it looked like he might have rouged his cheeks a little, too.

"*Mahtsai*," literally, get ahold of it, he said in Comanche as he came toward me, putting out his right hand.

"*Hah, maduahwe*," I said in greeting, and got up.

We shook hands. I introduced the old man to Audrey, and he shook hands with her, too. The three of us sat down, the old man in a straight-backed chair to our right. Lucy brought his coffee and handed it to him.

I was aware that it wasn't polite to do so without friendly preliminaries, but I launched right into the reason for our visit, anyway.

"That Vernon banker drilled a test well to look for oil on your place," I said in English to Nahnahpwa. I knew that he understood a fair amount of English, though he couldn't speak it. "We," I continued, motioning toward Audrey to my left on the couch, "want you to sign a paper, a lease, so we can drill a well and take the oil out. We will pay you money for signing."

"Kehe tsa nuh sokovi tuhka nabaa kaht," the old man said firmly and at once. I knew enough Comanche to get the meaning of what he'd said. *There is no oil underground on my land.*

There's got to be some mistake, I thought. I decided to try again. Maybe he hadn't understood me. Maybe I hadn't understood him.

"The banker," I said, again in English. "He came and looked for oil on your land. Isn't that right?"

"Puhiwi taibo tsa nuh sokovi ku tsah nah nabaa kaht," Nahnahpwa said with the same emphatic tone as before. *The banker said my land did not have any oil on it.*

"He came and looked for oil here, that banker white man," Lucy interjected in English to make sure that I'd gotten what her husband meant. "You are right about that. But the well was dry. He didn't find any oil. No two ways about it. There ain't no oil on this place."

"Are you sure?" I asked.

"Sure," Nahnahpwa said in English.

Audrey and I exchanged puzzled glances. "There's no oil?" she asked me.

"No oil," I said.

That was that. I asked the old couple how things were going for them on the farm. Lucy said that prices for their cotton and cattle were still low. They were hoping the situation was going to get better. The old man started talking about how they had changed from Republicans to Democrats. Lucy translated for us.

Nahnahpwa said that, before the Depression, Indians had voted Republican. They liked the Republican ballot symbol, the eagle. But now, the old man said, we vote for the rooster, the Democratic party's symbol. That is a bird we can eat, he said with a smile. Audrey and I laughed as soon as we understood what he'd said. It was a good joke, I thought, and with some truth in it, too.

Nahnahpwa motioned then to his wife, and she picked up a kitchen match and one of two hand-rolled cigarettes, twisted at the ends, that were on the table next to her chair.

"His fingers don't work good," Lucy said. "I roll his smokes." She handed the cigarette and the match to him.

The old man reached over and stuck the match to the hot stove. It popped and caught fire. He cupped a hand and lit the cigarette.

I knew that what he was doing was Indian medicine when he puffed four times on the cigarette without saying anything and, each time, twisted to blow smoke toward a different one of the four directions. I knew he meant to speak seriously.

Ritual finished, he started talking, pointing with his lips, in the Comanche way, toward Audrey. I couldn't get all of what he was saying and looked toward the old woman for a translation.

"Old Man says, 'You drop that black-headed woman for this one?'" Lucy said.

Audrey blushed, and I probably did, too.

"We're just good friends," I said.

He said something more. "Old Man says you made a good swap," Lucy translated. "He says a coyote come to him last night, when he was gittin' back to the peyote tipi from a call of nature, come right up close, talked to him."

The old man suddenly yipped four times to show how the coyote had sounded. It startled Audrey and me.

Then he spoke again. Lucy translated. "Old Man says you made a good swap."

That was all. He sat back in his chair and finished his cigarette. I waited a little while to make sure he was finished. Then I thanked them both, and Audrey and I got up and said our good-byes and left.

We could hardly wait until we got back in the car to talk about what Nahnahpwa had said about the oil. We avoided mentioning the rest.

"Does this mean," she said, shaking her head, "that the information Dub got about the oil was wrong and that he put out all that money for the other leases for nothing?"

"Down a rathole," I said.

"And Juanita got mad at him for no good reason, then?"

"Sure looks like it," I said.

"She came over this very morning, Juanita," Audrey said.

"She did?" I asked. "What for?"

"She wanted to rant at me about the oil deal, wanted me to let her have the leases Dub'd got signed. She even brought up the fact that our will says that if Dub and I died together or one after the other, Juanita gets everything," Audrey replied.

"You never told me that about the will," I said.

"Juanita said, 'Well, I'd get the oil leases if you died,'" Audrey went on. "And I said, 'Well, I ain't dead yet.' But she kept on about it. I'd put on a pot of pinto beans and was doing a washing, and she wouldn't even leave when I went out to hang my clothes on the line. She stayed right there in the kitchen, all sulled up, and started in on me again after I came back in the house. I finally just told her I'd had enough of it. I said Dub left me those leases, and they were mine—to retire on, someday. Well, it looks like I was wrong about that, now, the leases being no account. But, Okie, how come Dub got such bad information about the oil?"

"Marsh Traynor must have done it on purpose," I said. "He was mad as hell at Dub—and for good reason, I think. And it looks to me like, for revenge, Traynor sent his guy Jonesy to get drunk with Dub and act like he just let it slip that Traynor'd found oil out here, when he hadn't."

"Sent Dub on a wild-goose chase? Made him spend his money for nothing? Why would he do that?"

"Revenge, pure revenge," I said. "He wanted to get back at Dub in the worst way, and I know what for. Something always seemed fishy to me about that whole deal. No wonder Traynor just plugged the test well on old man Nahnahpwa's place—no oil. And no wonder, either, that he never tried to get any leases signed himself."

"Well, I was rich, there for about a minute," Audrey said, philosophically. "Have to keep eating beans and corn bread, I guess. And, speaking of food, why don't you go with me tomorrow night to the box supper out at Lincoln Valley School? I hate to go by myself, and you have always been mine and

Dub's best friend. The women out there are trying to get a new stove for the school hot-lunch kitchen, and I feel like I ought to help them."

"Well, if you want me to," I said. I knew that it'd probably cause talk, that some old biddies were likely to say that I was interested in Audrey. But I didn't think of it that way. I was focused on Juanita.

And I knew that I should look Juanita up and tell her what we'd found out about Dub's oil leases. But I wanted to put off for a while being the carrier of what would be to her such unwelcome news. I hated to be the one to tell her that the oil leases she was trying to get her hands on were not worth a dime, that the rumor Marsh Traynor'd put out about his oil strike was just a trick to get back at Dub for trying to frame him in a false deviant-sex incident with Poss Tatums.

TWENTY-THREE

It was just getting dark when Audrey and I got back to the Billings place. We found my dad in bad shape.

"Son just cain't seem to git easy," Grandma Dunn said, when Audrey and I came into the dining room. My dad was slumped over in the rocking chair near the stove, still in his plaid pajamas. His head was down, and his eyes were closed. "He tries the bed, and hit don't work, and he comes back to the rockin' chair," Grandma said.

Audrey went over and put her hand on my dad's shoulder. Grandma and I stood nearby. "Mr. Dunn, how are you feeling?" Audrey asked him.

My dad opened his eyes and raised his head. His swollen face was very pale. He looked at Audrey for a full minute before he answered, as if he wasn't at first sure of who she was.

"Tolable," he said, finally, and turned back to look at the woodstove. His breathing came in shallow and wheezing pants.

"Naw, you ain't, son," Grandma said to him. And then to Audrey, she said, "Pain's been gittin' worse all day."

"Do you hurt much, Mr. Dunn?" Audrey asked. She patted him softly on the shoulder.

"Gittin' rough," my dad said, "and I cain't git my breath good, neither." He began to cough, and each spasm caused him to double over and hold his ribs with his left arm. "Maybe if'n I could git on my feet," he said, and began to struggle to do so. Audrey helped him up. Being upright for a minute did seem to give him some relief. The coughing stopped, and he soon sat back down heavily, breathing hard.

He turned and looked up at me. "Okie," he said, "go and brang me that pint out from under the seat of my truck."

Grandma didn't say a word, and that probably surprised my dad as much as it did me. She obviously knew it was well past the time for complaining about my dad's drinking.

"I cain't put up with this here no more, without I have somethin' to deaden it," my dad said. He settled back in the rocking chair with a groan.

I went out to get the bottle. It was two-thirds full of cheap Echo Springs bourbon whiskey. I brought it back into the house and handed it to my dad.

"Git me some water for a chaser," he said, taking the bottle from me. I brought a glassful from the kitchen. He turned up the pint bottle of whiskey and gurgled down half its contents, then shuddered and stopped to get his breath. I handed him the water when he reached for it. He took a long drink of that and gave the glass back to me. Grandma stood silently, looking on with concern. She was obviously working hard at not saying anything. My dad turned the bottle up again and finished it off, then bent over and set it on the floor. He motioned, and I handed him the water glass. He finished it off, too.

"Might could lay down now, for a while," he said,

passing the glass back to me. "That orter knock me out like Lottie's eye."

Audrey and I walked him to the bed. He grimaced from the pain as we helped him stretch out on his left side. Audrey stacked up the pillows under his head, so he could breathe better, and pulled the blanket up over him to keep him from getting cold. At the stove, Grandma Dunn opened its hinged door and threw in a stick of oak wood from the stack against the wall.

"Dad, you want Audrey to bring you out a painkiller shot from the hospital?" I asked. "She can do it, if you need it." Audrey'd brought in her nurse carpetbag, but she'd earlier told me that she never carried morphine.

"Hit couldn't hurt to try it," he said, and closed his eyes.

TWENTY-FOUR

I spent most of Sunday with my dad. Grandma Dunn went in to church with neighbors. Audrey came out about noon and gave my dad another morphine shot. The pain in his chest was getting worse. Tough as he was, he needed the relief that the morphine gave him. But there were tradeoffs: deadened senses, in addition to cracked ribs, that made it hard for my dad to take deep breaths. He couldn't clear the congestion in his chest very well. His breathing got progressively more labored. Doc Watson had said that he might get pneumonia, and it began to seem like he had. He started running a fever.

Audrey stayed until Grandma got back. She left a supply of the painkiller and a hypodermic syringe with Grandma and showed her how to give my dad a shot.

The morphine did its job. My dad stayed in bed all afternoon, and then passed the night fairly well, though he coughed a lot and had a hard time breathing. Grandma and I took turns sitting up with him.

Monday, after my running and doing the chores around the place, I spent the day at the sheriff's office. Nothing much was going on. Stud went out to investigate a reported cattle theft. I twice tried to call Juanita, but couldn't get her. The gossipy telephone operator told me that she thought Juanita had gone to Lawton.

I spent a little of Cash County's scarce money— "frog hair," to Stud—and called long-distance to the State Crime Bureau in Oklahoma City to see if I couldn't rush up their report on Marsh Traynor's rifle and the bullets that had killed Dub and his folks. A snotty woman there told me that they'd just shipped the gun, the slugs, and the Bureau's analysis back to me by Mistletoe Express and that I would probably get them the next day.

"No, sir, that's not our practice," she said to me curtly, when I asked if she could tell me over the phone what was in the report.

I let Crystal off work early, so she could go home and bake the cherry pie that she said she was going to take to the Lincoln Valley box and pie supper that night.

I closed the office at five and drove out to the Billings place to check on my dad and Grandma Dunn. They didn't need anything. His condition was about the same, except maybe a little worse. Grandma Dunn gave him another morphine shot while I was there, and he got back in bed and fell asleep, despite his great difficulty in breathing.

"I been prayin'," Grandma Dunn said to me in a low voice in the kitchen before I left. "But, Okie, son, 'pears to me like you pore ol' dad ain't gonna make it too much longer. I got him to go to the Lord with me this mornin', and I think he's prepared hisself for what's comin'."

I hated to hear it, though I was afraid she was right. And I hated to leave the two of them alone, too, but I'd agreed to take Audrey to the box supper.

I told myself that there was nothing I could do, anyway, by staying home.

I'd spiffed up—my newest Levi's, ironed with a crease, black boots shined, white shirt, and black suit coat.

Audrey looked great when she came to the front door of her house to meet me. She was wearing a calf-length black-wool dress with white trim on the collar and pockets, black, low-heeled pumps, and a pert little black-felt hat that sat toward the back of her short and neatly waved hair. I stepped inside her living room as she opened the door.

Audrey handed me the pretty box of food she'd prepared for the box-supper auction. She'd taken a cardboard grocery case, like the kind that cans of tomatoes or corn come in, neatly pasted it over with a brightly sunflowered wallpaper, and after packing the supper food in it, had wrapped the box in crinkly yellow cellophane, gathered at the top and tied with a wide yellow ribbon.

I took the box in my left hand and, with my right, helped her on with the black-wool, full-length overcoat she took from the clothes tree by the door. Close to her as I did this, I inhaled a strong whiff of Evening in Paris perfume, and it affected me, made me feel a bit dreamy. Audrey looked at me kind of funny.

"You sure look nice," I said, to cover my embarrassment.

She picked up the nurse carpetbag from its place near the front door and put the wide strap of it over her right shoulder. I took her by that arm and guided her out the door and down the steps to the sheriff car.

It happened again. As soon as she got in what had been Dub's car, Audrey started to cry. "I just can't help it," she said. "I know he wasn't the best husband a woman could have, but I loved him, and I miss him."

"I know," I said. She stopped crying and wiped her eyes as I fired up the car and backed out of the drive.

"I fried some chicken, made a little potato salad, and put in a warm jar of the pinto beans I've been simmering for a couple of days," Audrey said after we headed north toward the highway. "I hope they get a good turnout at Lincoln Valley tonight."

"Crystal's bringing a cherry pie," I said. "Poor thing, I doubt that she and her folks and her little girl have enough to eat themselves at home, so I don't think she felt like she could afford to donate a whole supper."

"Well, it's a pie supper, too, not just a box supper; so that's all right," Audrey said. "That poor thing, though."

Lincoln Valley School was two miles east of Vernon and across East Cash Creek on the blacktop highway toward Comanche, then two miles north on a gravel school-bus road. It was getting dark as we arrived.

When we turned the corner at the white-clapboard, one-story frame school building, we could see that a pretty good bunch of people had already gathered. I drove into the gravel lot on the west side. It was nearly full—with model-A Fords and old-model Chevys, mostly, two or three old Dodges and LaSalles, a few later-model Fords, and about seven or eight wagons and teams. I parked on the south side of the lot, near the sturdy frame out-houses, one labeled Boys, the other, Girls, both two-holers, I knew, that had been built by WPA labor.

I went around and opened the door for Audrey and took the yellow-cellophaned food box from her. She got out with the nurse carpetbag and looped its strap over her shoulder. We cut across the rolled-dirt basketball court, where four teenage boys were getting in a few last shots before it grew completely dark outside. Three giggling grade-school girls were playing tag, back and forth over the vaulted ceiling of the cement cyclone cellar near the school's back door. We went around them, turned at the long-handled pump where five or six of the local men were finishing up a last smoke, and, after speaking to them, entered the school building from the front porch that ran the length of its east side.

The school looked just the same as when I'd gone there. I'd started the first grade at Lincoln Valley the year my folks lived on a 160-acre farm that my dad sharecropped, three-quarters of a mile east of the school. We'd milked a few cows and sold cream that year, herded turkeys, and raised some oats and a little cotton. After pretty much going broke, or broker, my dad had been like the cotton-picker who on a hot afternoon "heard the call" to preach. My dad had soon heard the call to get out of farming and start custom haybaling and trading cattle for a living. And somehow we'd made it through the years, although, a lot of evenings, Mama and Daddy and my sister and I hadn't had much more than corn bread and beans, greens, and clabber milk for supper.

Lincoln Valley's front door opened into the "little kids' room," with its four rows of desks, one for each of the four lowest grades that were still taught there by Mrs. Parton. She'd been my own schoolteacher, too, her first year out of normal school. She'd taught the little kids, and her husband had taught the big kids—grades five through eight.

As we went between the desks and the big blackboard in front and then along the sidewall, with its large, framed prints of George Washington and

Abraham Lincoln, I couldn't resist mentioning to
Audrey that, on my last day in school at Lincoln
Valley, Mrs. Parton had awarded me a new quarter
as a prize for being the first-grade pupil who'd read
the most books. I'd been really proud to win that
prize and more than glad to get the quarter, but I'd
liked even better having that tangible sign of Mrs.
Parton's approval.

I'd been her favorite, and I'd tried to make it to
school every morning as early as I could, back then, as
early as I could get my sister to leave our house. I
wanted to be the one, in winter, who got to help Mrs.
Parton make the fire in the woodstove in the back of
the room and, during other times of the year, clean the
blackboard and dust the erasers on the cement floor of
the porch out front, until the others arrived and Mr.
Parton clanged the bell in the yard at eight o'clock.

Audrey and I passed into the big kids' room
through the double doors that had been thrown
open, greeting people who'd already gathered
there—and there were a lot of them. The big kids'
room doubled as an assembly hall. There was a foot-
high platform across the front of the room that was
used as a stage. An oilcloth curtain, painted with an
idyllic landscape and advertisements for Vernon
businesses, could be rolled down in front of it on
ropes from the ceiling. On the west wall was an
oversize print of George Washington, again, and one
of equal size of President Franklin Roosevelt.

The room was pretty well packed. Some people
were gathered in clusters, visiting. Others had begun
to take seats, either one behind the other, in the four
rows of school desks that had been shoved back a
ways, or in the wooden folding chairs that had been
set up in front of them and around the walls.

Coming into the big kids' room, Mr. Parton's room,
which, of course, had seemed much larger when I was

a first-grader, made me vividly recall that he'd been killed that past Halloween night when he'd crashed his Indian motorcycle on the highway coming back from Vernon. Nobody knew what was going to become of Mrs. Parton. She was sure to lose her job the next school year. Country school boards liked to hire husband and wife teams who could live in the teacherage together on roughly one and a half salaries. A single woman teacher could hardly make a living on what she was paid.

It was Mrs. Parton herself, dressed in an ankle-length black-crepe dress, an old lady's square-heeled black shoes, and a black basketlike straw hat over gray-streaked hair drawn back in a bun, who met Audrey and me as we approached the stage with Audrey's pretty yellow supper box. Mrs. Parton beamed in a pleased but reserved way when she shook hands quite formally with me.

"That's your old pupil, Nancy," one of the women standing near her at the stage said to Mrs. Parton, and, then, to us, "How are you, Okie, Audrey?"

I don't think I'd really ever focused, until then, on the fact that Mrs. Parton had a first name, and I would have died right there before I could have called her Nancy, myself.

"He was, indeed," Mrs. Parton said to the woman, and, turning slightly to include Audrey, added, "This was the brightest little boy you can imagine. He just loved, just really *loved*, to read. What a gorgeous box you've made, Audrey."

She took it, then, and stepped up onto the stage to set it with the other boxes and baskets and pies that would be auctioned off later.

"What she said must have made you feel awfully good, Okie," Audrey said.

"I'd give her the quarter back to say it again," I said.

We hung our coats on wall hooks for the kids' wraps, though Audrey kept her nurse bag. We mingled with the crowd, shaking hands, saying hello, visiting a little. Stud and his wife, Ethel, a matronly woman in a flowered rayon dress with a high neck, were there. So was poor lean and ungainly Crystal. She had come alone—in a freshly washed and ironed cotton dress, and her graying brown hair was brushed to a sheen and held in back with a tortoise-shell barrette. I told her she looked nice. Her plain face turned red, and she looked down quickly at the oiled-wood floor.

We of our little sheriff's posse, plus Audrey, all found seats on the same row of wooden folding chairs near the front, as good old Judge Dowlin, pasty-faced and stocky, came along the center aisle and greeted his way, left and right, up to the stage. He was wearing the usual greenish three-piece suit, maybe the only one he had. He was still sporting the tan-blond wig that should have had a little gray in it to match the real hair of his temples, and which appeared, I noted, to have drifted slightly off center, a tiny bit over toward his right ear.

"Ladies and gentlemen," Judge Dowlin called, loudly enough to be heard over the final visiting back and forth by the crowd and the scraping of chairs as the last people sat down just in time to have to get to their feet again. "Please join me in the salute to Old Glory," the Judge said.

He turned to face the American flag, which was to his left and toward the back of the stage. The blue Oklahoma flag, with the green Osage shield on it, was on the opposite side. We all stood, faced the Stars and Stripes, and began the pledge in unison, extending our right arms, palms up.

"Please remain standing for the invocation," Judge Dowlin said before we could sit back down.

"Miz Parton, would you please lead us in prayer?"

My old teacher remained in her place in the front row. "Let us pray," she said. Heads bowed. "Lord, we thank you that in America we can still get together like this as a community. We thank you for these people, for this school, and for the children who go here. You know our needs, Lord. We ask you to bless us. Be with the sick and the shut-ins, Lord. Be with those who are going to bed hungry tonight. Be with our missionaries on foreign fields. And now, Lord, bless the food we will partake, here, to the nourishment of our bodies and us to Thy service. In Jesus' name we pray. Amen."

"Amen," people said, here and there. They coughed and cleared their throats, scraped their chairs, and sat.

Miz Parton came forward to the old upright piano at the back of the stage, and Judge Dowlin led us in song. We sang "My Country, 'Tis of Thee" and "There's a Long, Long Trail Awinding."

Called up to the stage by the Judge, the raggedy Fitzgerald family—man, wife, and nearly grown son and daughter—sang a couple of numbers. It was well-known that Fitzgerald was bad to drink, and people said that he sometimes beat his wife. But he really knew the old-time songs. He played the mandolin, she the guitar, and the four of them brought tears to a lot of eyes as they movingly harmonized on "Tracing Little Footprints Through the Snow" and "Over the Hill to the Poorhouse."

Judge Dowlin then began to coax people to come up to the stage for the cakewalk. "It only costs a nickel, folks, and you can win one of these fine homemade cakes," he said, gesturing toward a low bench on which two chocolate and two angel food cakes rested.

Little by little, enough people came forward and

paid their nickels to fill the dozen places that had been chalked and numbered on the stage floor in a circle. At the Judge's signal, Mrs. Parton struck up a lively "Camptown Ladies" on the piano. The cake-walkers began to circle, stepping gingerly to the beat, until, again on the Judge's signal, the music stopped, and he awarded the first cake, one of the angel foods, to the red-faced farmer in overalls who was found standing on number eleven, which the Judge'd earlier drawn from folded slips of paper in his hat. There were shouts of congratulations to the winner and moans and groans from the losers, and that group straggled back to their seats to make room for the next bunch that felt lucky.

The cakewalks continued until all four prizes had been awarded. And then it was time for the auction to begin. Judge Dowlin asked a couple of the women to row up the twenty or so boxes and the ten or so pies along the front of the stage. I wasn't surprised when he began with Audrey's box. If there'd been a prize for the most attractive one, hers would surely have won it.

"Now, no one knows, of course, whose this is; we're biddin' blind, as usual," Judge Dowlin said in his orator's voice, "but if the lady who made this is as lovely as this wonderful box, and if the supper it contains is even half as delightful as the whole thing looks, the man who buys it and gets to eat it with the little lady is going to have a memorable evening."

I knew whose box it was, of course. And I was just as sure that I was going to be its buyer, whatever the cost. I was looking for a memorable evening, too, like the Judge had said. But I had no idea just how memorable it was going to turn out to be.

"All right, boys, y'all know it's all for a good cause—helping the Lincoln Valley ladies buy a new hot-lunch stove," Judge Dowlin said. "What am I bid? Who's going to start it out with a quarter?"

"Four bits," I called out. I didn't look at Audrey. I knew my face was red.

"Four bits!" Judge Dowlin said. "Boys, does the sheriff know something we don't? Hope you're not spending the *county's* money, Okie." People laughed. I probably turned redder.

"Fifty-one cents," somebody in the back yelled.

"I'll go fifty-two," Stud called out, right by me.

Stud, for God's sake? He was jabbing me, I knew. I turned and gave him one of my bad-hombre looks. "What in the corn bread hell?" I said in a low voice across Audrey and Crystal. "We're partners, remember."

"That's cattle, stud," he said. "Not box suppers."

People closest to us laughed again. I had decided not to worry that some silly people might say that I was sweet on Audrey when they found out for sure that it was her box I was so set on buying.

"Sixty," I called, raising the bid by eight cents at one jump. There was a kind of buzz in the crowd.

"Sixty-one," the guy in the back yelled.

"Okie?" the Judge questioned, pointing at me.

"Six bits," I said.

I got the box, and it turned out that seventy-five cents was, by far, the highest price paid for a box all night.

And, to top it off, about midway through the auction, I bought Crystal's cherry pie, too. I'd made her tell me which one it was. The guy in the back had bought the box Stud's wife had brought, and, when all the boxes and pies had been sold, she carried it back there to eat with him. Stud bought the second prettiest box of the evening, one wrapped in red-and-green paper saved from Christmas, and he got up and went over on the east side of the room to join its maker. She turned out to be a stern Church of Christ lady with no makeup, middle-aged, mother of four kids—and the kids ate with Stud and her. It was good enough for him, to my way of thinking.

Audrey, Crystal, and I stayed where we were and turned a trio of empty folding chairs around to face us for tables.

Crystal set the box that held her cherry pie on the chair in front of her and opened the top and turned it back. It was just a plain white bakery-type box, tied with a thin blue ribbon. She wouldn't have won a prize for the box, but I knew that her pie would deserve to. It smelled great, and you could see the red cherries and filling through the slits in the rich, sugared crust on top and along the deliciously ooz-ing lines where the pie had already been cut into six slices. Crystal took a knife, two forks, two small, chipped china plates, and two frayed but clean white napkins out of a flour sack that she'd earlier put on the floor by her purse and laid them out alongside the pie box.

"Looks good enough to eat, Crystal," I said. Another Will Rogers.

She blushed and looked down. "Not much to it," she said. "I just used some cherries that I canned last summer and some welfare-commodity flour and lard and sugar. Pert near used up all our sugar, though."

Audrey had chucked her nurse bag under the fac-ing chair on which she'd placed her own supper box. She carefully folded the ribbon and cellophane from the box for use again. She spread a cloth across the chair in front of me and laid out the crispy brown fried chicken—two wings, a thigh, and a breast—as well as three golden pieces of corn bread with the kind of brown crust I loved, a pint jar of her great, practically patented, potato salad, and another pint jar that held a goodly portion of the pinto beans that she'd slow-cooked with ham hocks. She spread open a little cellophane package of sliced onions to eat with the beans and set it out, together with two sets of white paper plates and napkins and a couple of nice stainless forks she'd packed.

Crystal looked over at this feast, and I thought she was going to faint from obvious hunger.

"I already had supper before I left home," I said. I was lying, of course.

"Me, too." Audrey had seen the way Crystal had looked at the food, the same as I had.

"I just want a wing," I said. "And maybe a slice of corn bread. And then, mainly, I'm going after that cherry pie."

"I was thinking the same thing," Audrey said. "Here, Crystal, you better not let this go to waste." She pushed the middle chair with the most food on it a little farther over in front of Crystal.

"Y'all sure?" Crystal said.

"You bet," I said.

"Here, let me put some of these red beans on a plate for you," Audrey said, "and some of this potato salad, the chicken breast—I hope you like white meat, Crystal—and some corn bread. How's that look?" She handed the full plate and a fork and napkin to the poor woman.

Crystal didn't wait to answer. She started right in on the beans, each time scooping up as much as the fork would hold and barely pausing long enough between mouthfuls to take a breath and dab at her mouth a little with the napkin.

Audrey and I took up a fried chicken wing and began to nibble. We were both moved by the woman's pitiful hunger.

Crystal concentrated solely on the red beans, like she didn't want to mix tastes, and rapidly ate every last one on the paper plate. She paused a moment then, and took a breath, preparing to turn, next, it looked like, to the potato salad, fried chicken, and corn bread.

But before she could go on, Crystal suddenly lurched jerkily to her feet, groaning and holding her stomach.

"What is it Crystal?" I said, alarmed by her actions and contorted face. "What's the matter?"

"I gotta go out back," she mumbled. Her face was turning greenish. "I'm sick."

"You want me to go with you, darling?" Audrey said, concerned.

"No." Crystal barely squeezed out the word, then wheeled and fled the room in a stiff-legged and jerky gait. People stopped eating, momentarily startled, and watched her leave.

"Too much on an empty stomach, you think?" I said to Audrey.

"She didn't look right. I'd better go see about her." Audrey stood up and, with one hand, pulled her nurse bag from under the chair. With the other she picked up one of Crystal's cloth napkins. "I'll wet this at the pump," she said.

But just as Audrey headed toward the connecting door, two excited red-faced grade-school boys rushed through it and into the room.

"It's a woman, y'all, fell down on the ground!" one of the boys shouted. "Come quick!"

"Havin' a fit, looks like," the other boy yelled, out of breath with alarm, too.

There was a rush to the door, behind Audrey. I joined in. We crowded into and through the little kids' room, then pushed on out the front door of the school building, off the porch, and into the yard.

One of the boys who'd sounded the alarm shouted as we all got outside, "This way!"

On the south side of the school, a quarter way to the toilets, Crystal lay facedown, twitching, on a patch of brown Bermuda grass. Audrey was already opening her nurse bag as she quickly knelt and lifted Crystal's head.

"Audrey's a nurse; give her room," I said to the people who'd started bunching around the convulsing woman. I took the cloth napkin from Audrey and handed it to a man nearby. "Here, wet this at the pump," I said. He jumped to do so.

Audrey opened Crystal's clenched jaw and stuck her finger a little way down the back of her tongue. Crystal heaved, but little came up.

"Gag response!" Audrey was reciting to herself, heedless of the rest of us. "Needs an emetic!"

She grabbed a bottle out of her bag, unscrewed the cap, and practically poured the thick brown liquid down Crystal's throat. This caused almost an immediate gush of vomiting, and Audrey jerked Crystal over on her left side to give the mess that came up clear exit.

"Beans," a woman said. She was right.

The vomiting ended quickly. Audrey turned Crystal on her back again and, seizing the wet napkin I'd taken from the man and handed to her, rapidly wiped Crystal's mouth and face as the poor woman began to twitch again.

"Gotta stop the convulsions!" Audrey was talking to herself again. "Phenobarbitol!" She jerked a hypodermic syringe from her bag and, with quick rummaging, a small vial, too.

"Oxygen! She needs oxygen!" Audrey said to herself as she rapidly filled the syringe. Turning to me, she commanded, "Quick, Okie! Artificial respiration, like she was a drowning victim."

I jumped to straddle Crystal's frail form, quickly raised her arms above her head, and began at once to pump down on her bony chest with both hands and then release the pressure in lifesaver rhythmic strokes.

Audrey rapidly pushed up Crystal's right sleeve to bare thin biceps and quickly gave her the injection.

Crystal's jerking subsided, and, after a time, she opened her eyes. I stopped the artificial respiration and moved off her. Crystal looked blankly at Audrey for a moment and then at me.

"I'm sorry," she said in a small and pitiful voice.

"Don't talk," Audrey told her. Then, turning toward some of the men hovering nearby, she said, "Would some of y'all carry her out and put her in the backseat of Okie's car? We've got to get her to the hospital, fast."

Stud was one of those who carried her. I felt sick, myself, my chest aching. I was out of breath from the exertion.

Audrey went to the car with Crystal. I ran back inside the school building to grab up our coats and things, then rushed back to the car to haul poor Crystal to the hospital. Other people, talking in hushed tones, started to leave, too.

I rapidly dumped the coats and Audrey's wallpapered box-supper box in the trunk of the sheriff car. But I kept out the pint jar that still had about a quarter of an inch of red beans in it. I screwed its lid on tight and put the jar in my coat pocket.

I jumped in the car, quickly started it, and began to back out. Audrey was in the backseat, cradling Crystal's head in her lap.

"Don't eat any of those beans at home, or let anyone else," I said to Audrey, swiveling my head back toward her as I sped out of the parking area and into the road. "I want to get what's left of this batch tested."

"I won't." Audrey had obviously been thinking the same thing I had.

We rushed through the night toward the Vernon Hospital.

TWENTY-FIVE

It was near midnight before I got back home. I'd stayed at the hospital to be sure Crystal was stabilized and waited there until Stud could go get Crystal's mother to come in and sit up with her.

As I pulled into the Billings place, there was a light on in the dining room, where my dad's bed was. A tan Dodge coupe sat in the driveway. I figured this had to be my sister, Alene, and her husband, Jake. I'd called them the preceding day to tell them that Dad probably wasn't going to make it, and they'd obviously driven straight through from Long Beach.

I was right. Alene met me as I came through the kitchen into the dining room and gave me a good hug. Jake had already gone to bed.

"Poor old Daddy's been having a hard time, Okie," Alene said. "I'm glad you called us when you did."

He was awake and partly sitting up in bed, propped up with pillows. Dad's breathing was more labored than ever. Grandma Dunn was standing at the foot of his bed.

"He's been runnin' a bad fever, off and on,"
Grandma Dunn said to me. "Twicet, I give him
aspereens, and I been rubbin' his face and hands
with a cold rag."

My dad looked over toward me. "Light me a
Camel, Okie," he said, "and put it in my mouth."
He could hardly breathe, but he still needed a
smoke.

I went around to the other side of the bed, near
the window, and picked up the pack on the bed
stand, shook out a cigarette, and lit it with one of the
kitchen matches that were bunched there by the
pack. I took a drag to get the fire going and puffed
the smoke right out again. It burned my eyes. I put
the cigarette in my dad's lips, and he took as deep a
suck on it as his congested lungs would permit, then
coughed out the smoke instead of inhaling it. I
jerked the Camel back out of his lips, leaving a bit of
the paper stuck there, so he could get his breath.

Dad's coughing was what Audrey had called
"unproductive." He couldn't take deep enough
breaths to get under the congestion and bring anything up. His chest stayed tight, his breathing ever
more difficult.

"Son, you know you orter lay off them cigarettes," Grandma Dunn said, but there was no con-
viction in her voice. She was across the room by the
stove.

"Never orter started, Ma," he said between
wheezes and coughs, "but hit's too late now." He
motioned, and I put the cigarette to his lips, so he
could take another pull on it, which he did, and then
started coughing all over again.

"Oh, Daddy, don't give up," Alene said, tossing
her light hair out of her face as she came to the bed,
on the opposite side from me, and leaned over him
and caressingly pushed the hair back from his fore-

head. "It's you that always said things are never as bad as you think."

"Well, hit turns out, sister, sometimes they is," he said. "And sometimes they even worse'n you thank. This here's one of them times, looks like."

He motioned me away with the cigarette. The last drag had cost him too much. I snuffed it out in the bronze ashtray in the shape of a horseshoe that sat on the bed stand.

Grandma Dunn opened the stove door and poked in two heavy sticks of oak, even though, for me, the room was already overheated.

"We love you, Daddy," Alene said, her voice breaking. Tears came to her eyes.

"I know that, hon," he said, "and you know you ole daddy loves you, too. I love y'all kids."

It was the first time either of us had ever heard him say anything like that, except when he was on a crying drunk and pretty much out of control.

"I know I perty much made a failure," he went on.

"Don't say that, Daddy," Alene said. "You always made us a living. We never went hungry."

"You've been a tough son of a bitch, Daddy," I said, a kind of crazy thing to say, but I meant it as the best compliment I could think of. He *had* been tough. He could do anything he put his mind to, and he'd never been afraid of anything or anybody.

"Not tough enough for this," he said. "But I always did the best I could, and that's all a *mule* can do."

He began to grimace with pain and put his left arm over his chest.

"Grandma, can you give him another shot?" I said.

"You don't think hit's too much?" she asked, coming over to the bed.

"He ought not to hurt," I said. "No need to."

She went and got the hypodermic and sucked the morphine solution into it from a little glass vial, the way Audrey had taught her. With Alene's help, my dad turned on his side a little, facing me. Grandma pulled his pajamas down some and stuck him in the hip.

"Maybe you can get some rest, now, son," Grandma said.

"Y'all, too," he said, and closed his eyes.

Alene, Grandma, and I huddled over by the stove and talked in whispers. "Y'all go on and get a little sleep," I said to them. "I'll doze here in this rocker and sit up with him tonight."

Grandma fixed me up another morphine shot for later in the night and laid the syringe on a towel on the bed stand. The two of them went to bed. I blew out the coal-oil lamp on the table over by the door to the bedrooms, leaving only the one on the dining-room table, which was pushed back to the south wall. Then I slumped down in the rocking chair in front of the stove and fell asleep almost at once.

It was not quite two in the morning when my dad roused a little and began to cough again. He didn't seem to be in pain, but he was uncomfortable and breathing hard.

"Okie?" he rasped.

"Right here, Daddy," I said, and jumped up and went over to his bedside. "You need something?"

"Nightmare," he said. And then he went on, like he wanted to talk and erase his dreams, or his thoughts. "You know, Okie, you been wrong about Marsh Traynor. He ain't never gonna shoot nobody in the back. Might kill a feller, if'n he needed killin', but Marsh shore'n hell would be starin' the guy in the face when he pulled the trigger." He stopped to get his breath.

"I think you're probably right, Daddy," I said. "I've got some tests coming in from the City tomorrow, and I think they're going to eliminate his gun."

"'Nother thang, son," my dad went on. "'Pears to me like you jes askin' fer it, playin' that Juanita, Dub's sister."

"I think you might be right about that, too, Daddy."

"They's a spell on that woman," he said. "She gonna rern you, Okie, if'n you don't let her go."

"You want a painkiller shot?" I asked.

"Naw, I thank I kin make it a while longer," he said, and settled back and closed his eyes. I returned to the rocker after a time and soon dozed off again.

About two hours later, my dad woke up again, and, this time, the pain was back, and his breathing was worse than ever.

"You want that shot, now?" I asked, going around the bed and picking up the hypodermic.

"You know how to do it?"

I told him Grandma Dunn had shown me. I pushed him over a little, gritted my teeth, and stuck him in the hip. I was never meant to be a doctor.

"What time is it?" he asked. "Still dark out."

I pulled out my pocket watch. "Five minutes after four," I said.

"This is the time of night that old people die," he said, matter-of-factly. I knew he knew what he was talking about. He'd sat up all night a lot of times with old people who hadn't made it to sunup.

"I wish it'd get light," he said. He turned and looked out the east window toward where the sun would appear in another couple of hours. But he was not going to see it, and I felt he knew that, right then. He turned back and closed his eyes.

I took his rough old right hand in both mine and got a good grip back in return. It was more intimacy than we'd ever shared before. His breathing got slower and slower, and then, finally, as his grip went slack, stopped altogether.

I waited, still holding his hand. And then he suddenly thrashed around and willed himself back awake, and alive, again. His eyes opened wide with fright. He gripped my hand once more and began to take labored breaths. But his eyes soon closed again. His breathing slowed. His grip on my hands loosened, and he stopped breathing again.

Tough as a boot he was, though. He shook himself back alive once more. And again there were the frightened eyes and the tightened grip. I let go his hand and laid it across his stomach and began to talk to him soothingly while I patted his bony shoulder with my right hand and smoothed back his hair again and again with the other, like I'd seen my sister do, earlier.

"You'll be all right," I said, like I was talking to a child. "Just go to sleep. You're tired out. Just go to sleep. You'll be all right." I bent over and kissed him on the forehead. He never knew it, so neither one of us had to feel embarrassed about that tender act.

My dad's body relaxed. His breathing first grew faint, then stopped altogether. And this time, it never started up again.

"You'll be all right," I said, tears in my eyes. "Just go to sleep." He did.

Things are never as bad as you think, except, every now and then, they're worse.

TWENTY-SIX

Grandma Dunn, first, and then Alene and her husband, Jake, got up and learned the news. Alene took it particularly hard.

"Hit were a blessing, hon," Grandma said as she brought us some coffee. "Ain't gonna have to suffer no more, now." I figured she was right.

Grandma began to put together some clothes to lay my dad out in.

It was too late to go back to sleep. I put on my running clothes. I didn't feel much like running, but I ran, anyway. I was glad I did. It helped me clear my thoughts and decide on everything that had to be done.

I ran all the way south to old man Nahnahpwa's gate and then back. The weather had turned overcast and cold. There was a north wind, and before I got back home a freezing mist was falling. It looked like we were in for the first of the two or three ice storms that always hit Oklahoma every winter. I'd loved them as a kid. You could skate on the roads in your shoes, or get a fast and scary ride by grabbing hold of someone's back bumper.

But I wasn't a kid anymore. If I had been, I'd have been an orphan. I was feeling like an orphan, both my folks being dead. *You're on your own in this world, Okie,* I told myself as I jogged along. And I felt all right with that. In a strange kind of way, I felt like a authentic adult, maybe for the first time, fully. I knew I wasn't as tough as my dad, but I figured I was tough enough.

Back home, I ate a quick bite with Alene and Jake and talked about funeral arrangements. Jake helped me, and we made short work of the chores. Then my morning of arrangements, reports, and amends began.

I drove first to Vernon's little hospital. Crystal was asleep when I got to her room, and her mother was dozing, too, in a chair near the bed. The old lady roused herself when I came in.

"Hi, Okie," she said, and got up and went over and rubbed Crystal's face with a wet cloth that she took from the nightstand.

"How's she doing?" I asked.

"Got her knocked out, now," Crystal's mother said. "Poor thang suffered a restless night, but the doctor says she's come through the worst of it."

Stigler-Martin Funeral Home was my next stop. I felt like it was becoming a kind of gruesome second home for me. Greg Martin said he'd send a hearse for my dad's body. I picked out a casket, and we set the service for the next afternoon at the First Baptist Church.

Stud Wampler was at the office when I finally got there and had finished up feeding the prisoners. He broke down and cried when I told him about my dad.

He was embarrassed about crying in front of me, and I was embarrassed for him, and he quit pretty quickly.

"Hudge Dunn was a good sumbitch, Okie, and

you can always think good of him," Stud said when he'd straightened up. "But he was just wore out and used up."

Mistletoe Express called to say two packages had come in for us. I sent Stud to the corner to get them while I cleaned the cells, upstairs. He was soon back, and the packages, as we'd figured, contained Marsh Traynor's semiautomatic .22 rifle and the four spent bullets that had killed Dub Ready and his folks. Folded in the box with the slugs was the official report of the State Crime Bureau. All the bullets, the report said, had been fired by the same rifle, but Traynor's wasn't it. This news, of course, was no surprise.

I sent Stud on an errand to the country to look for a different semiautomatic .22 rifle. We thought we knew where it might be found.

Doc Watson telephoned me at the office, as I had asked him to do when I'd awakened him late the preceding night and ordered testing of any remaining residue in Crystal's stomach and in the leftover portion of beans that I'd taken him.

"You were right, Sheriff," he said. "Strychnine."

"The beans?"

"You were right about that, too, Sheriff. Somebody really poured the strychnine to that pot of beans, enough to kill a whole pack of coyotes. You could clearly tell that, even from that little dab of beans you brought me."

I changed the subject to one I'd been thinking about for days.

"Doctor," I said, "pay close attention, now, to what I'm about to say to you. You hear me?"

"Yes, I do, Sheriff." He sounded apprehensive.

"I'm going to put two separate choices to you," I said. "The first one is this: you stop peddling morphine, and paregoric, too, when it's not appropriate, or I'm going to send you to the pen."

Doc Watson made a noise like the beginning of a denial.

"Dare say a word except in agreement, and you're damned sure headed to the pen," I said. "Now, you choose."

There was a long pause, then finally, he said, simply, "All right." But he said it too hesitantly to suit me.

"Say it like you mean it! And you'd *better* mean it," I said.

"All right," he said, more firmly. "I mean it."

"Here's the other choice," I said. "Either you go up to Norman and enroll in that detoxification program and get *yourself* off of morphine, or I'm going to run you out of town. Now, you choose again, but don't give me any shit."

Again there was a long pause, and when he finally spoke, he didn't bother with a denial of his addiction. "Who would take care of my practice?" he asked plaintively.

"You can get someone to come down from Lawton two or three days a week while you're gone. But I expect you to be in Norman within a week. You hear me, sir?"

"I do hear you," he said, then added, "and I'll make the arrangements and do it."

I telephoned Audrey next. She was at home, taking the day off—and with good reason. I told her to burn the rest of that batch of beans in her garbage barrel.

"How awful," she said, knowing the implications. "Are you going to do it today?"

"Pretty soon," I said.

"Want me to go with you, Okie?"

"I've got to do it myself, Audrey," I said. "My dad always said, 'If you hadn't a-wanted to work, you oughtn't to have hired out.' It's my job."

"Good luck, Okie," Audrey said before she hung

up. "I'll be thinking about you, and I'll come by the funeral home this evening to see about you." I appreciated that.

The mail came, and I got my third report of the day. It wasn't a surprise, either. The University of Oklahoma Student Disciplinary Committee begged leave to inform me that the appeal of my law school suspension for slapping a professor had been denied. I could apply for readmission two full years after the occurrence of the incident.

Stud came back with the rifle—a .22 semiautomatic. It had been in the harness room of the barn, right where we'd suspected it would be. Over behind some salt blocks and a couple of cottonseed-meal sacks, he said. Not hard to find.

"We'll send it to get tested," I said. "But I don't think there's much question about what the answer's going to be."

I told Stud about Doc Watson's report.

I told him about the University of Oklahoma report, too, and added, "Looks like I'm stranded in Oz."

"No, Sheriff stud, cheer yourself up," Stud said, in the nasal W.C. Fields voice. "The situation is not nearly so adverse as you might think. Like that Wizard book says, you and Toto would otherwise have to go and live the rest of your lives in *Kansas*!"

I told Stud that I was going to the bank, and then I'd be back to pick him up. I told him that I wanted him to go with me for support for the last act of the day, but only to sit in the car.

A freezing rain was coming down steadily, and Main Street was already iced over and slippery. I didn't pull into the curb, for fear I wouldn't be able to back out again. I double-parked. Sheriff's privilege.

Marsh Traynor bounded out of his chair and came out to greet me as soon as I entered the bank. He put a big arm around my shoulders. "Okie, I'm sure sorry about you dad," he said.

I thanked him for the sentiment, which I knew he felt, then let myself be ushered into his small desk area, behind the low, oak rail.

"What can I do for you, Okie?" he said after we'd seated ourselves. He was bellowing, as usual, and tellers were turning to look.

"Well, I came to apologize."

"Figured you'd get around to that eventually," he said. "You're a man."

"I mean, I was investigating you for killing Dub Ready and his folks," I said.

"I know what you mean." He rubbed a hand over his bald head.

"I know about that horrible Poss Tatums frame and the unsuccessful blackmail attempt on you," I said. "I know about your fake oil-strike scheme, having your man Jonesy tell Dub that you'd hit oil on old man Nahnahpwa's place, when you hadn't, just for revenge on Dub. That was a mean thing to do, tricking Dub into spending his money for nothing, but I guess it wasn't a crime. And I also know that you had no part in any of the murders."

"I could have told you that," Traynor blared. "For God's sake, I was huntin' ducks up north by the Park on the Saturday mornin' that Dub Ready was killed. Lum Mallow's boy, Gus, was with me. I'd a told ya that if you'd a ask me."

"I know," I said. "I just came to beg your pardon. I simply want to say that I'm sorry."

"Pissed me off, sure, Okie, but it's under the bridge," he said. "You was just tryin' to do your job the best way you knew how. I still believe in ya, son, and you gonna make us a sheriff. I don't have no doubt about that."

TWENTY-SEVEN

Stud and I drove to the nice little rock home on Main, across the highway and north of the Truckers Cafe. I pulled around to the rear of the house when I saw Juanita coming out her back door just as we arrived. She had a Coke in her hand and was heading out toward her little corrugated-tin barn and horse lot. When she saw me, she stopped in the dead grass, midway between dwelling and barn, and waited.

I parked behind her Jimmy pickup and shut off the motor. Stud sat tight. "Take a deep breath, stud," he said. I did.

I got out then and walked over toward Juanita. She was in Levi's, a man's striped shirt with the tail out, and an unbuttoned, heavy wool sweater over that. Her long black hair was loose and unbrushed. There were dark circles under her eyes. Her normally flawless white complexion was flushed pink, her cheeks both chapped. She was wearing no makeup or lipstick.

"I knew you'd be coming, Ray Lee, as soon as I heard about poor Crystal," she said when I came up to her. Her eyes were bleary and looked dilated, even though the day was overcast and sunless. "I hate Crystal getting sick, most of all. I never wanted that."

"You wanted the rest, though," I said.

"I can't deny that."

"For God's sake, Juanita, your parents!" I said. Tears came to my eyes. I'd just lost my last one. "Greed, was that it?"

"I guess you could say that was it, mainly. Money—I was always desperately short of it. You can put that in your report, Ray Lee."

"And Dub, you were laying for him in that slough," I said. "You didn't go to Cookietown to buy hay. You'd already bought plenty of hay from Pilkington."

"You're right," she said quietly. "I never went to Cookietown."

"And Dub's last words," I said. "I thought he was telling us to watch over you and Audrey, but I figure, now, that he was saying for us to watch over her and watch *out* for you."

Juanita didn't say anything. I went on. "Killing Dub and, then, the strychnine-poisoning of Crystal that you meant for Audrey, was that just greed, too? You were their heir, in the will that you got them to get drawn up."

"Pretty much greed, yes. Money again. I'm an awful, awful person."

"You didn't used to be," I said. Tears kept coming, but I didn't even bother to be ashamed about that. I reached out to take her hand, the left one without the Coke. She pulled it back. "Your folks beat y'all up, I know, and I found out that your father abused you," I said.

"Hush, Ray Lee. Truth is that I've never been much account. You just didn't know."

My hat and raincoat and her sweater were getting soaked. Her black hair was wet and growing icy on top. Neither of us paid any attention.

"Juanita, I wanted to help you," I said. "I wanted to make things like they used to be."

"Can't make a silk purse out of a sow's tit, Ray Lee."

"Ear."

"That either," she said. She looked off through the cold rain toward the barn. "Now *is* the winter of our discontent, Ray Lee. I'm the one who should have played poor Richard III. I've, all my life, been deformed, like him."

"I've got to take you to jail, Juanita."

"I know it," she said. "But let me go to the barn, first, and put some oats out for Sugar before we leave." The wet mare was standing in the corner of the lot nearest us, her head up and her eyes constantly on Juanita.

"All right," I said. "Do it."

Deliberately, slowly, she poured out onto the grass some of the Coke she'd been holding and, afterward, held the plump, pale green bottle up at eye level and was apparently satisfied to see that it was only about half full.

"I've got to take care of business, Ray Lee," she said quietly, and started toward the barn. I let her go. She entered the barn through a wooden residence-type door and closed it behind her.

"Everything all right, stud?" Stud called to me.

I walked over to the car.

"Just give her a few minutes," I said. I stood by Stud's open window, as the cold rain kept coming down, wetting me even more and him, too, some.

After a while, I said, "All right, it's time to go see about Juanita."

Stud got out, and we walked over to the little barn's door. It was latched from the inside and wouldn't open.

"Juanita," I hollered. There was no answer.

I nodded to Stud, and he kicked the door open, tearing the small interior lock from its screws.

Juanita was lying on some loose alfalfa hay on the dirt floor of the barn, next to a stack of bales. Her face was terribly contorted, her eyes were wide-open, fixed, as if in fright, and her arms and legs were oddly splayed out this way and that. The Coke bottle she'd carried lay on the floor, empty, and next to it was another bottle, a pint-sized dark and rectangular, medicine-looking bottle with a skull and crossbones and the word, "poison," noticeable on its white label.

I knelt quickly and found that there was no pulse in Juanita's neck. Neither her terrible appearance nor the fact that she was dead affected me as much as it should have. I'd had time to steel myself, prepare myself.

Stud picked up the dark poison bottle and examined the label.

"Strychnine," he said. "Left over from killing coyotes, my guess."

"Well, let's go in her house," I said, "and call Stigler-Martin one more time, and Doc Watson, too."

Audrey came down to the Stigler-Martin Funeral Home that night, as she'd said she would. I'd been looking for her, and I left Grandma, Alene, Jake, and the others with my dad's body in the viewing room and went out to the reception area to meet her.

There were a lot of people in the funeral home.

"Well, at least Greg Martin's doing all right," Audrey said.

"Catching 'em faster than he can string 'em, my dad would say," I said. "Greg ought to put me on commission."

"You want to go get some coffee, Okie?" she asked.

I did. We slid our way down to the Truckers Cafe in the sheriff car. Irma hugged me when we entered, and I let her. I sank into her about a couple of inches. She was choked up and didn't say anything, but the embrace said enough. I appreciated her sadness about my dad's death.

Audrey and I shook out our hats, my wet Stetson and her equally soaked little black, medium-brimmed felt, and hung them and our raincoats on the clothes tree near the cash register. We sat down across from each other at one of the metal tables.

Irma brought the coffee, then left us to go and serve other customers. Audrey had already heard about Juanita. I filled her in on the melancholy details. We sat in glum silence.

After a time, I also told Audrey about the bad news that had come in the mail that morning from the university.

"Looks like I'm stuck here in Oz," I said, unable at the moment to think up a new cleverness.

"And a lot of us Ozmanians are glad of it, too," she said, and reached across the table, put her hand on mine, and squeezed. "You know what they say, Okie: 'One door closes, another one opens.'"

"Who's 'they'?"

"Us Ozmanians, I think," she said.

Look for *Easy Pickin's*

by Fred Harris

Coming soon from HarperCollins Publishers

It was the Saturday morning before Easter 1938, which that year fell on April 17, that a human body hurtled out of a diamond-clear sky and slammed right down in the middle of a flat Oklahoma oatfield.

The day'd been windy, but the local weekly, the *Vernon Herald*, couldn't have made a headline out of that. It wouldn't have been news. The wind always blew in southwest Oklahoma. Stud Wampler, my main deputy, liked to say that chickens in that part of the country had to carry rocks to keep from getting blown away.

The relentless "Dirty Thirties" wind of the awful Dust Bowl years, just earlier, had scooped up and hauled a lot of Oklahoma on down to Texas, dribbling out lives and dreams along the way. But 1938, itself, had not been a Dust Bowl year—like 1936 and 1935 were. Thank God! And by Eastertime, we hadn't had any tornadoes, yet, in those parts.

So, you didn't have to be the Cash County sheriff—as I was, right then—to deduce that no diabolically fierce wind had suddenly snatched up the human body in question from somewhere else and then dumped it like a tree limb in the center of that wavy, green field of newly headed oats.

The field belonged to two uncles of mine, Uncle Joe Ray and Uncle Leroy Vanderwerth, bachelor brothers of my dead mother. The common saying around there about people like those two was that "their eggs got shook." They'd been all right, twenty-one years earlier, in 1917, when they'd left Vernon to go and fight in the Great War in Europe. But they'd come back from the hell-hole trenches "shell-shocked," as people said, never the same again.

The two brothers, slat-slim and all knees and elbows, were as poor as Job's turkey, as mama would have said. They made a living the best they could on a 160-acre Indian lease–hunting and fishing, raising turkeys, selling cream and eggs, and making home-brew beer. Periodically, they sold dressed squirrels door to door in Vernon for the asking price of two bits, but now and then had to take fifteen cents because times were hard, and a lot of people didn't any more have an extra two bits to spare than my uncles did.

There was nothing addled about the uncles' report of what they'd found in their field that Saturday before Easter.

"Hit were one of our coondogs, that blue-tick named Willie, that set up sich a ruckus out in them oats," Uncle Leroy said.

"That uz how we-uns got the idee somep'n other was out there," Uncle Joe Ray said.

They'd followed the coondog's baying and run out, barebacked and barefooted, to the oatfield in front of their old house to see what was the matter. Finding the dead body, they'd looked it over quick-ly, then turned right around and jogged back to the house and jerked on their shoes—without socks, I could see—and their wrinkled gray workshirts, outside the suspenders of their ragged Blue Bell overalls. They'd hitched up their mismatched team–a big bay horse and a little sorrel jenny—to their frail wagon and careened off, north, to the rented house where I was batching—the old Billings place on the east side of Vernon—to bring me the news.

Telling me about what they'd found, the two of them were as excited as coon dogs that've run an armadillo in a hole. Spraying snuff juice through snaggled teeth and talking over each other in their high-pitched voices, they blurted out their story, answering when I asked, that the victim was dead, when first discovered.

"Dead as Aint Idy's cat, Okie, hon," is the way Uncle Leroy put it.

I'd been named after these two uncles. My real name was Ray Lee Dunn. But my dad had put the nickname, Okie, on me when I was little because I was born on November 16, Oklahoma statehood day. The nickname had stuck. I was going on twenty-seven that Easter weekend of 1938, Oklahoma, thirty-one.

"Deader'n ol' Woodrow Wilson," Uncle Joe Ray said.

The uncles were puzzled about one thing, though, and when they mentioned it to me, both of them, like twins, ran their bony fingers through spiky gray hair, which looked to me like they'd whacked on it, themselves, maybe with their pocket knives. They'd been unable to decide whether the victim's death had come prior to the fall, or as a result of it.

"Acourse, hit don't make a heap a difference to the corpse," Uncle Leroy said.

"Deadfall or fall dead, all the same to the faller," Uncle Joe Ray said.

And fall was sure enough what that body had

done, no doubt about it. Right out of a cloudless sky. It had neither been blown nor, as it turned out, carried to where it'd landed in the Vanderwerth brothers' oatfield—about three miles southeast of the county-seat town of Vernon, Oklahoma, twenty some-odd miles this side of Red River.

The train of events that led up to the body falling from the sky had begun two days earlier, though, on the Thursday before Easter. That's the day a small covey of three strangers showed up, separately, in our little town—all of them somehow connected, time would show, to the Case of the Unknown Girl, as Stud Wampler would soon start calling it.